the Pongwiffy stories

This omnibus edition published in Great Britain in 2017 by Simon and Schuster UK Ltd
A CBS COMPANY

Pongwiffy: A Witch of Dirty Habits first published by A & C Black (Publishers) Ltd 1988
Pongwiffy and the Goblins' Revenge first published under the title *Broomnapped*
by A & C Black (Publishers) Ltd 1991

1 3 5 7 9 10 8 6 4 2

Simon & Schuster UK Ltd
1st Floor, 222 Gray's Inn Road
London
WC1X 8HB

www.simonandschuster.co.uk

Simon & Schuster Australia, Sydney
Simon & Schuster India, New Delhi

A CIP catalogue record for this book is available from the British Library.

PB ISBN 978-1-4711-6738-6
eBook ISBN 978-1-4711-6739-3

Printed and bound by CPI Group (UK) Ltd, Croydon, CR0 4YY

MIX
Paper from
responsible sources
FSC® C020471
www.fsc.org

Simon & Schuster UK Ltd are committed to sourcing paper that is made from wood grown in
sustainable forests and supports the Forest Stewardship Council, the leading international forest
certification organisation. Our books displaying the FSC logo are printed on FSC certified paper.

FSC logo are printed on FSC certified paper.

CONTENTS

WITCHES AND FAMILIARS

SOURMUDDLE & SNOOP

PONGWIFFY & HUGO

SHARKADDER & DEADEYE DUDLEY

AGGLEBAG & IDENTIKIT
BAGAGGLE & COPICAT

SLUDGEGOOEY & FILTH

MACABRE & RORY

BENDYSHANKS & SLITHERING STEVE

GAGA & BATS

BONIDLE & SLOTH

SCROFULA & BARRY

GREYMATTER & SPEKS

RATSNAPPY & VERNON

the Pongwiffy stories

A witch of Dirty Habits

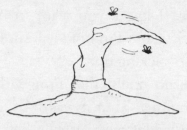

CHAPTER ONE
entertaining

'**W**itch Sharkadder! My old friend!' cried Witch Pongwiffy, opening the front boulder with her very best welcoming smile firmly fixed in place. 'What a lovely surprise. Welcome to my humble cave. My, you do look nice. Is that a new hairdo, or have you had some sort of terrible shock, ha ha? Just my little joke. Come in, come in. Let me take your hat.'

She seized the tall hat, gave it a respectful little brush and waited until Sharkadder's back was turned before booting it into a dark corner.

'It's hardly a surprise if you knew I was coming,' remarked Sharkadder coldly, advancing into the cave. 'I know you want to be my friend again, Pongwiffy, but I'm not at all sure I want to be yours. So stop sucking up.'

There was no doubt that Pongwiffy was being revoltingly smarmy – but it was for a good reason. She and Sharkadder were usually best friends, but they had recently had one of their quarrels, and Pongwiffy was anxious to make amends.

'Oh, you're not still thinking about that silly old quarrel, are you? Come on, Sharky, let bygones be bygones. Have a look at my new cave. I only moved in last week. You're my first guest.'

Sharkadder stared around distastefully.

Pongwiffy's cave wasn't a pleasant sight. It had shocking damp problems for a start. Slimy green moss grew on the walls, and the floor was a sea of muddy puddles. The broken-down furniture wasn't so much arranged as thrown in any old how. Thick black steam belched from the horrible-looking slop which bubbled and heaved in the cauldron.

'Well, sit down, Sharky. Make yourself at home,' fussed Pongwiffy, removing Sharkadder's cloak and dropping it into a slimy pool.

2

'There's nowhere to sit,' observed Sharkadder.

'You'll have to use that cardboard box. I haven't sorted out the chairs yet. That's the trouble when you've just moved in. It takes ages to get organised, doesn't it?'

'You've never been organised,' said Sharkadder. 'What's that terrible stink? Smells like skunk.'

'It is,' said Pongwiffy cheerfully. 'It's tonight's supper. My speciality. You'll love it. Skunk stew. I'll just give it a stir.' And she took a large ladle and poked at the gurgling goo in the cauldron.

'Oh,' said Sharkadder, wishing she'd stayed at home. 'Skunk stew. Really?'

'I knew you'd be pleased,' said Pongwiffy. 'Now, tell me truthfully. How do you like the cave? It's a little damp, I know, and perhaps a bit small, but it was very cheap. Of course, it's a nuisance being in Goblin Territory, but I can't afford anything better at the moment. What do you think of it?'

'It's a dump,' said Sharkadder. 'It's a smelly little slum. It's not fit to live in. It's squalid and yucky. It's the worst cave I've ever been in. It suits you.'

'It does,' agreed Pongwiffy, pleased. 'I feel it's me. It's a pity about the Goblins, though. I'll tell you about them later. Now then. How much stew for you, Sharky?'

'Er – about half a teaspoon,' said Sharkadder hastily. 'I had a huge lunch. And I think I've got a touch of tummy trouble.'

'Nonsense,' said Pongwiffy, relentlessly approaching with a huge, greasy plateful. 'Get that down you. That's a lovely perfume you're wearing. Don't tell me – let me guess. "Night In A Fish Factory", right? And I do *so* like the new hair-style. It really suits you. Brings out the beakiness of your nose.'

'It does, doesn't it?' agreed Sharkadder, finally coming round after such an onslaught of flattery. She scrabbled in her bag, took out a small, cracked hand mirror and examined the frazzled mess with satisfaction.

'I've got some new hair rollers,' she explained. 'Little hedgehogs. You warm them up. Not too much, or they get bad-tempered and nip. Just enough to send them to sleep. Then you wind the hair round, and wait for them to cool. And it comes out all curly, like this.'

'Beautiful,' nodded Pongwiffy through a mouthful of stew. 'You always look so nice, Sharky. I don't know how you do it.'

'Yes, well, I do try to take care of myself,' said Sharkadder, tossing her tangles and applying sickly green lipstick. 'You'd look a lot better yourself if you washed once in a while. And changed that disgusting old cardigan.'

'What's wrong with my cardigan?' asked Pongwiffy, clutching the offending garment to her bony chest.

'What's right with it? It's got holes. It's got no buttons. You've spilt so much food down it, you can hardly see the pattern. It looks like it's been knitted with congealed egg. Want me to go on?'

'No,' muttered Pongwiffy sulkily.

But it was true. Pongwiffy's sense of personal hygiene left a lot to be desired.

'As for those flies that buzz around you all day long, it's time you swatted them,' added Sharkadder, enjoying herself.

'Swat Buzz and Dave? Never!' declared Pongwiffy, aghast at the idea. She was fond of her flies. They circled round her hat, shared her food, and slept on her pillow at night.

'Look, let's not talk about flies and cardigans. You'll never change me, Sharky. I like the way I am. Try some stew. I made it specially.'

'I can't. I haven't got a spoon,' hedged Sharkadder.

'What on earth do you need a spoon for? Slurp it from the plate, like I'm doing,' said Pongwiffy, demonstrating.

'No, I want a spoon,' insisted Sharkadder.

Pongwiffy sighed and went to the sink. Sharkadder watched her crawl under the table, duck under the cobwebs, heave a heavy wardrobe to one side and kick a dozen cardboard boxes out of the way.

'I don't know how you bear it,' said Sharkadder with a shudder. 'Don't you ever tidy up?'

'Nope,' said Pongwiffy truthfully, returning with a spoon.

Sharkadder eyed it with a critical frown. 'It's dirty,' she observed. 'What's all this crusty stuff?'

'Last week's skunk stew,' explained Pongwiffy. 'No point in washing it, seeing as we're having the same. Now, what was I going to tell you? Oh yes. My new neighbours. You see . . .'

'I want a clean spoon,' interrupted Sharkadder.

The strain of being a polite hostess was suddenly more than Pongwiffy could bear.

'Honestly!' she shouted. 'You're such a fusspot sometimes. I go to all the trouble of inviting you for supper, and all you do is . . .'

7

Just at that moment, there came an interruption. There was an ear-splitting crash, and the walls shook. The Goblins in the cave next door had arrived home. You should know quite a bit about the Goblins Next Door, because they feature rather a lot in this story.

The Goblins Next Door consisted of a whole Gaggle. A Gaggle is seven Goblins. These were called Plugugly, Stinkwart, Eyesore, Slopbucket, Sproggit, Hog and Lardo. They had moved in a week ago, about the same time as Pongwiffy, and had already caused her no end of aggravation.

This seems a good time to tell you a little about Goblins in general. Then you can decide for yourself whether or not you would care to live next door to them.

The most important thing you should know about Goblins is this: they are very, very, *very* stupid. Take the business of their hunting night – Tuesdays. That's when they hunt. It's Traditional. Whatever the weather, every Tuesday they all troop out regardless and spend from dusk till midnight crashing about the Wood hoping to catch something. They never do. It's common knowledge that the Goblins are out on Tuesdays, so everyone with any sense stays safely indoors and has an early night.

The Goblins are always surprised to find the Wood deserted – but they'd never think of changing their hunting night to, say, Thursdays, thus catching everyone unawares. That's how stupid they are. Of course, you could forgive them their stupidity if they weren't so generally all-round horrible.

After the futile hunt, Goblins always have a party. The party is always a flop, because there's never anything to eat, and invariably ends with a big fight. Goblins like fighting. It goes with their stupidity, and the Tuesday night punch-up has now developed into a Goblin Tradition. It's a silly one – but then, all their Traditions are silly. Here are a few more, just to give you the idea:

Painting Their Traps Bright Red; Bellowing Loud Hunting Songs Whilst Walking On Tiptoe; Stomping Around In Broad Daylight With Faces Smeared With Soot, so they won't be noticed; Wearing Bobble Hats, even in a heatwave, To Stop The Brains Freezing Up; Cutting The Traditional Hole In The Bottom Of The Hunting Bag, so that whatever goes in immediately falls out again.

Right, that's enough about Goblins in general. Let's now get back to the Gaggle in the cave next door to Pongwiffy.

All Goblins are great music lovers, and Pongwiffy's new neighbours were no exception. They kept her awake at all hours, playing ghastly Goblin music at very high volume. Goblin music sounds rather like a combination of cats trapped in boxes, burglar alarms, and dustbin lids blowing down the road, so you see what she had to put up with.

It was most unfortunate, then, that the Gaggle Next Door chose the very night that Pongwiffy was entertaining Sharkadder to supper to hold their Official Cave-Warming Party.

Just take a look at the following:

7 Goblins make a Gaggle

3 Gaggles make a Brood

2 Broods make a Tribe

1 Tribe makes life unbearable.

The Gaggle next door had invited no less than *two entire Tribes* to their cave-warming – and that, if you can't work it out for yourself, is eighty-four Goblins! They all arrived at the same time, singing. Can you imagine?

> *'A hundred squabblin' Goblins*
> *Hobblin' in a Line,*
> *One got stuck in a bog, me boys,*
> *Then there were ninety-nine . . .'*

they howled joyfully, pouring into the cave. Next door, Sharkadder leapt from her cardboard box, sending the plate of skunk stew crashing to the floor.

'My new neighbours,' explained Pongwiffy, scooping the spilt stew on to her own plate. 'I'll eat this if you don't want it.'

> *'Ninety-nine squabblin' Goblins*
> *Hobblin' out to skate,*
> *One went under the ice, me boys,*
> *Then there were ninety-eight . . .'*

warbled the Goblins relentlessly, stomping around in their hobnail boots and beating their warty heads against the wall. A small avalanche of stones rained down on Sharkadder's new hairdo. A large spreading crack indicated that the ceiling was about to fall in.

'Stop them! Stop them making that dreadful noise!' howled Sharkadder, trying in vain to protect her curls.

> *'Ninety-eight squabblin' Goblins*
> *Hobblin' down to Devon,*
> *One got chased by a bull, me boys,*
> *Then there were ninety-seven . . .'*

droned on the Goblins, and Pongwiffy's favourite poison plant keeled over and died on the spot.

Then the ceiling *did* fall in. There was a groaning, grinding noise, and down it came with a huge crash, burying both Pongwiffy and Sharkadder under several tons of rubble. Luckily, they're Witches – and Witches are tough.

'Sharky? Where are you? Are you all right?' called Pongwiffy, crawling out from under a large slab of granite and peering through the murk at the fallen boulders littering the floor. There was a moment's silence. Then the overturned cauldron gave a heave, and Sharkadder emerged, shaking with fury and covered from head to foot in skunk stew.

'Oh dear,' said Pongwiffy. 'Sorry about that.'

'I'm never speaking to you again, Pongwiffy!' hissed Sharkadder, and she ran weeping from the cave.

'Ninety-four squabblin' Goblins
Hobblin' out to tea . . .'

Pongwiffy picked her way through the rubble and staggered out, gasping for air. She was just in time to see Sharkadder mount her Broomstick, which was saddled outside, and zoom off, splattering the tree-tops with skunk stew and screaming shocking curses. Pongwiffy's own Broom was propped where she had left it, fast asleep as usual.

'One got choked by a crumb, me boys,
Then there were ninety-three . . .'

Pongwiffy marched up to the Goblins' front door, which was, to be exact, their front boulder, and rapped sharply.

There was a sudden pause, followed by muffled mutters of: 'Fink dat's Uncle Slobbergum?' 'No, he's already here.' 'Where?' 'In de soup. He just fell in it.' 'See who it is, Stinkwart.' 'Where's Plugugly? Answering the boulder's his job . . .' and so on.

Finally the boulder rolled back, and Pongwiffy found herself staring into the repulsive, lumpy countenance of Plugugly, the biggest Goblin.

'Yer?' he growled, scratching unpleasantly and glaring at Pongwiffy with small, red, piggy eyes.

'How many more? How many more verses to that wretched song?' demanded Pongwiffy in a shrill voice.

'Derrrrrr . . .' Plugugly thought deeply, his brow creased in concentration. Maths wasn't his strong point.

'Wait dere,' he said, and vanished to confer with the others inside. Pongwiffy tapped her foot impatiently while the whispered arguments went on, and grimly fingered the Wand which hung on a dirty string around her neck. Eventually Plugugly returned.

'Ninety-two,' he said. 'Yer.'

'Over my dead body,' Pongwiffy said.

'If you like,' Plugugly said.

'Do you realise,' snapped Pongwiffy in her firmest no-nonsense voice, 'do you realise that you have brought my ceiling down? You've quite ruined my supper party. You've upset my stew, not to mention my best friend. I haven't slept a wink for days – not since you moved in. Every night I have to listen to your caterwauling. There's a limit to my patience. Who d'you think you are anyway?'

'Goblins,' said Pluguly with the confidence that comes from having the body of a bolster topped with a face like an old, squeezed tea bag. 'Goblins. Dat's what we is. And we does what we likes.'

'Oh you do, do you? And suppose I put a spell on you, and *banish you from this cave*?' Pongwiffy produced this ace from her sleeve with an air of triumph.

'Derrrrrr . . . wait dere,' ordered Plugugly, and retreated inside again. Pongwiffy waited. After a few moments, he returned.

'You better come in,' he said.

It was grim and gloomy in the Goblin cave. The air was thick with dense smoke curling from the torches jammed into crevices in the walls. There was an overpowering smell of Goblin, which threatened to overwhelm even Pongwiffy's own personal odour – and that's not easy, as you would know if you ever stood downwind of her. Holding

15

her nose, she peered around.

One hundred and eighty-two small, red, piggy eyes peered right back at her. Everywhere she looked, there were Goblins. They sneered from the shadows, scoffed in the corners and gibbered and jeered in the gloom.

Some wore the Traditional Goblin Uniform, which is baggy trousers held up with braces, and, of course, the time-honoured bobble hat. Others wore stolen leather jackets dripping with chains and studs. These were members of an outlaw Goblin Brood from a grotto high in the Misty Mountains. They called themselves the Grottys, and would dearly have liked to own motorbikes. So far, however, they only possessed one rusty tricycle between them which they took turns falling off.

There were lizard-like, scaly Goblins, grossly fat Goblins, hairy Goblins, bald Goblins, drooling Goblins, scraggy little weaselly ones with long noses, tall spindly ones with short noses, and Goblins with humps, lumps and bumps in the most surprising places. All of them wore huge boots, all had small, red, piggy eyes, and all looked and smelt as though they had crawled out of a blocked-up drain.

'Roight, boys!' said Plugugly. 'Bit of 'ush if you

please. Dis ole witch wants a word.'

The Goblins sniggered and nudged each other.

'Yes,' said Pongwiffy severely. 'I do. I'm getting very tired of you lot. In fact, I'm not putting up with another minute of it. You've brought my ceiling down. My best friend's not speaking to me and my hot-water bottle's punctured. It's a disgrace. In fact, I'm seriously thinking of casting a Spell of Banishment on you. What do you say to that, eh?'

To her surprise, none of the Goblins looked the least bit worried. In fact, several of them tittered. One even *yawned*.

'So I'm warning you now,' continued Pongwiffy uneasily. 'Any more noise, and that's it. Whoosh, gone, the pack of you.'

'Let's see yer do it,' challenged Slopbucket, sidling closer.

'Her her her! Yer, let's see yer do it!' was the general cry.

'I will!' threatened Pongwiffy. 'I will, too. Unless you promise to remove your boots and whisper from now on. Do you?'

'NO!' came the howled chorus. 'NO! NO! NO!' And they cheered and began a slow handclap as Pongwiffy seized her Wand and held it aloft.

Now, that was very odd, for a Witch's Wand is guaranteed to put fear into the heart of any Goblin. Brutes, bullies and thoroughgoing pests that they are, they have one disadvantage, apart from being stupid. They Can't Work Magic.

Pongwiffy gave her Wand a little shake to make sure it was working. Green sparks crackled at the tip and it began to hum. All was well.

'Here I go! One Banishing Spell coming up!' And she began the chant.

> Blow you winds with all your might.
> Blow these Goblins from my sight.
> Where you blow them I don't care.
> 'Long as they're not here, but there!'

Nothing happened. The Goblins nudged each other, grinning. Pongwiffy frowned at her Wand and tried again.

> Blow you winds with might and main.
> Goblins drive me quite insane.
> Take them to a cavern deep
> So I can get a good night's sleep!

Still nothing. Then she became aware of wheezing chortles and horrible strangled snorting noises. *The Goblins were laughing!*

They fell about, digging each other in the ribs and hooting with mirth.

'I don't understand it,' mumbled Pongwiffy, staring aghast at her Wand, which had ceased to spark, or even hum, *and had a knot in it*! 'It's always worked before . . .'

'It's quite simple, really,' explained Slopbucket, mopping his streaming eyes. 'It's like this, yer see. *We bin banished already!* To this 'ere cave. So you're stuck wiv us. Har har har!'

'*What?*'

'True as I'm standin' 'ere, ain't it, boys? It were a Wizard what done it. At our las' place. 'E comes complainin' about the noise, see, just like you. We gives 'im a bit o' lip, see, an' in the end 'e declares us a – what were it again?'

'Public Nuisance!' roared the Goblins with great pride.

'Yer, dat's it. Public Noosunse. So 'e gives us the boot 'n' banishes us 'ere. An' 'ere we gorra stay. Fer ever. *So your feeble ole spells won't work!*' Which was true. Wizard Magic is strong stuff, and not easily undone.

'Her her her!' wheezed Plugugly, shoulders heaving. 'Worra laugh, eh?'

'No,' snapped Pongwiffy coldly. 'It isn't.'

'Tell yer what,' continued Plugugly. 'We can come to a – wassit called again?'

'Compromise?' said Pongwiffy hopefully.

'Yer, dassit. Compromise. You don't come round 'ere again complainin', and we won't smash yer place up. 'Ow's that sound? Reesnubbo?'

It didn't sound reasonable at all. Pongwiffy glared into his grinning, stupid face and debated whether to punch him on the nose or move out the next day.

She moved out the next day.

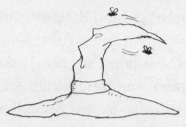

CHAPTER TWO
House Hunting

'It's very kind of you to put me up, Sharky,' said Pongwiffy to Sharkadder one week later. They were in the kitchen of Sharkadder's small cottage in Witchway Wood at the time.

'That's all right, Pong,' lied Sharkadder with fingers crossed behind her back. She had, of course, forgiven Pongwiffy for the disastrous supper party. After all, it hadn't been her fault, as Sharkadder had to admit when Pongwiffy had grovelled long enough.

However, there was a limit to friendship.

Pongwiffy had been sleeping in Sharkadder's spare room for over a week now, and was showing no signs of moving out. Sharkadder was a houseproud Witch, as Witches go, and Pongwiffy was a Witch of Dirty Habits.

They were sitting at the breakfast table. Sharkadder, who was on a health kick, had made do with a glass of fresh newt juice. Pongwiffy, who wasn't, had worked her way through two plates of lice bites, three griffin eggs, a pile of toast with jellyfish jam and thirteen cups of hot bogwater. She had also finished the trifle from the night before.

'I suppose I'll have to start looking for a place of my own one day,' said Pongwiffy, licking the trifle plate clean.

'Oh, really? What a pity,' said Sharkadder insincerely. 'I'll just go and get the paper, then. We'll see if there's anything suitable.' And without even bothering to put on her lipstick, she ran out of the door with what Pongwiffy considered to be indecent haste.

Pongwiffy finished up Sharkadder's newt juice and went to the cupboard to raid the biscuit tin, keeping a close eye on Dead Eye Dudley. Dudley was Sharkadder's Familiar – a huge, battered black tomcat with one yellow eye, a crooked tail and a very, *very* bad temper.

Rumour had it that Dudley had spent one of his nine lives as ship's cat on a pirate ship. This would account for the eyepatch he wore, and his habit of growling strange, piratical sayings. Everybody was terrified of Dudley, except Sharkadder, who loved him dearly. Right now he was asleep on the hearth-rug, claws flexing as he dreamed of chasing rats in the hold and wailing sea shanties under a tropical moon.

Pongwiffy hastily crammed the last three icky bikkies into her mouth and wondered whether Sharkadder would notice if she cut herself a piece of that delicious-looking fungus sponge hidden on the top shelf. Before she could decide, she heard Sharkadder's footsteps hurrying down the path. Hastily she scuttled back to the table and repositioned herself, humming a casual little hum.

In came Sharkadder with *The Daily Miracle* under her arm. She glanced disapprovingly at the pool of spilt bogwater, crumbs, broken eggshells and other assorted droppings at Pongwiffy's feet, and signalled to her Broom. It leapt to attention and briskly proceeded to sweep the mess under the rug, giving Pongwiffy's ankles several sharp raps in the process.

Pongwiffy's own Broom came hurrying up to join in. This cleaning business was quite a novelty. Normally, it never did a thing between flights except sleep. Pongwiffy briskly kicked it back into the corner. If there was one thing that annoyed her, it was a domesticated Broom.

Sharkadder tutted and opened the windows to let in some fresh air. Fond as she was of her friend, there was no denying that Pongwiffy's odour tended to get a bit overpowering at times. She cleared a space in the breakfast debris and spread out the newspaper, running a finger down the **FOR SALE** column.

'Now then, let's see. Here's one: **Igloo. North Pole. Apply Yeti, Greenland.**'

'Too far,' said Pongwiffy firmly. 'Too cold.'

'Hmm. All right, what about this? **Pretty little cottage with roses round door. All clean and shiny. Lovely views.**'

'Yuck! Sounds awful,' shuddered Pongwiffy.

'Here's another one, then: **Cave. Goblin territory. No ceiling. Otherwise perfect.**'

'That's where I've just come from! No thanks.'

24

'Well, that's all there is today. Oh, wait a minute, this sounds interesting. Listen: **Tree House for sale. Own landing platform. Ideal for high-flying witches. Every mod con.**'

'What's that mean?'

'Really, don't you know anything? Modern Contraptions, of course,' said Sharkadder, who was a bit of a know-all at times. 'It sounds ideal,' she continued. 'We'll go and take a look right away.'

'What – now?' bleated Pongwiffy, eyeing the toaster sadly.

'Certainly. We must strike while the iron is hot,' replied Sharkadder, and bustled away to put on her lipstick.

By the time Pongwiffy had exchanged her filthy old dressing gown for her filthy old cardigan and chased the spiders from her hat, the iron had cooled considerably – but they went anyway.

'I don't like it,' muttered Pongwiffy, eyeing the distant tree house doubtfully. It looked very high up indeed, and Pongwiffy is one of those Witches who can only stand heights if there's a Broomstick clamped firmly between her knees.

'Nonsense. You can't even see it from down here,' said Sharkadder.

'That's what I mean. It's too high. I wish I had my Broom.' Pongwiffy hadn't been able to persuade her Broom to come. It had become friendly with Sharkadder's, and wanted to stay behind and help sweep up.

When Pongwiffy argued, it merely swept away and returned with a copy of the Coven Rule Book, pointing a bristle at the rule which said, 'Daytime flying on Broomsticks is strictly forbidden.'

'Well, you haven't, and that's that,' snapped Sharkadder. She was beginning to suspect that Pongwiffy had no intention of leaving – ever. Which was true. Pongwiffy enjoyed the breakfasts too much. 'You'll just have to climb the rope ladder, same as anyone else,' she added.

'Can I borrow your Wand?' asked Pongwiffy hopefully. Hers was still in a state of trauma after trying, unsuccessfully, to cancel out Wizard Magic.

'Certainly not!' Sharkadder was shocked at the request. Wands are not to be used lightly. Serious Magic is what they are intended for, and planting lazy Witches in treetops could not be considered as Serious. Besides, they weren't supposed to borrow Wands. It was against The Rules, like daytime flying of Broomsticks.

'You go first, then,' said Pongwiffy.

'No,' said Sharkadder, who didn't like the look of the rope ladder either. 'No, I'll spoil my make-up. I'll stay down here and catch you if you fall.'

'Thanks very much,' Pongwiffy snapped crossly.

'Not at all,' snapped back Sharkadder even more crossly, and made a note to break friends as soon as Pongwiffy was settled.

Swallowing hard, Pongwiffy caught hold of the flimsy ladder, and set her foot on the bottom rung. It swayed alarmingly.

'What's the matter? Scared?' jeered Sharkadder, seeing her hesitate.

'Who, me? Certainly not,' said Pongwiffy, and started up the lower rungs at a bold run.

She had only scrambled a little way when she began to slow down. She already sensed that she was unnaturally high. The air felt colder. A chilly gust of wind blew up her cardigan, and she gripped the thin ropes more firmly.

'How much further?' she called down, not liking to look up.

'Lots,' came Sharkadder's voice from below. She sounded shockingly far away. 'Keep going, you've hardly started!'

Pongwiffy gulped and forced herself to move on up. Her knees scraped on the tree trunk as she climbed, bits of moss and tree bark fell in her eyes and her cardigan kept getting hooked up on the smaller branches.

A fat wood pigeon flew past her head, staring in puzzlement before flying away. Pongwiffy risked a glance up. The tree house seemed even further away now than it did from the ground.

'Hurry up!' called Sharkadder. 'I can't wait all day, I've got important things to do!'

Her voice rang with a worrying new echo. Pongwiffy looked down, and trembled at what she saw. Sharkadder had turned into a midget. From this angle, her body had disappeared, and only her small, upturned white face with the slash of green lipstick could be seen.

Pongwiffy's hat fell off, and she stifled a squawk as she watched it drop dizzyingly through space. Her arms ached, her stomach churned, and she felt sure she was catching a cold. The wind blew more strongly, and a hoarse cooing filled the air. The wood pigeon had returned with a gang of friends in order to watch her ordeal. They settled on the outlying branches of the tree and watched with keen interest as Pongwiffy hoisted herself still higher.

'Mustn't look down. Mustn't look down,' Pongwiffy mumbled through dry lips as the wind dragged at her rags. The tree, which looked so stout from the ground, suddenly felt very unstable, as though it might topple over at any minute.

'Yoo-hoo! Pong!' Sharkadder's voice floated up. It might be important. Perhaps she was trying to warn Pongwiffy of some hazard she hadn't yet seen. Unwillingly, Pongwiffy looked down.

'I've got your hat, Pong! It's quite safe!' called Sharkadder, waving it merrily. Pongwiffy nearly wept. 'You're nearly there now. Keep going!'

Pongwiffy was now so high that it was hard to make out Sharkadder's words. Snivelling, she dragged herself up a few more rungs while the posse of wood pigeons sniggered unsympathetically. One of them took off, hovered just above her head and dropped something rather unkind on her shoulder. The rest thought that was hysterically funny. The only one who wasn't laughing was Pongwiffy.

All too aware that she was running out of steam, she looked up. To her relief, Sharkadder was right. She had nearly gained the top rung. The sturdy tree house platform was so close now. Desperately, she

clawed at the ropes. One step . . . two steps . . . three
. . . nearly there . . . almost . . . another rung . . .

'BOO!' said a voice. Staring down at her was a
small green Tree Demon. It was crouched on all
fours, looking over the platform edge. In its hand
was a sharp axe. Pongwiffy very, *very* nearly let go
with the shock – but not quite.

'What d'you want, Witch?' hissed the Tree
Demon, waving the axe.

'A rest,' said Pongwiffy.

'Not a chance. Not in my house. I don't like
Witches.'

'What do you mean, *your* house? This isn't *your*
house. It's for sale.'

'Not any more it ain't. Bought it this morning.
Paid a deposit. Early Tree Demon gets the worm,
eh? Now, if you'd just move your hand a bit . . .'

And so saying, the Tree Demon took its sharp
axe and cut through the rope ladder.

There was silence over the breakfast table the
following morning. Sharkadder was daintily sipping
her newt juice and picking at a plateful of scrambled
ant eggs. Pongwiffy had her right arm in a sling, and

was staring gloomily at the stale crust which had been set before her. The standard of breakfast was definitely declining.

There was no doubt about it – she had outstayed her welcome. Sullenness hung in the air like a cloud. Dead Eye Dudley was sitting with his back to everybody, and even the Brooms were sulking. Pongwiffy had lectured hers at great length about its refusal to leave the house the previous day, never mind The Rules – who was the boss anyway? – and Sharkadder's had come out in sympathy. At length, Pongwiffy broke the silence. Somebody had to.

'Are we going to look at any more houses today, then?'

Sharkadder shrugged. 'You are. I'm not. *Hours* we wasted at the Witch doctor's yesterday. All for a little bruise on your elbow. You made me late back for Dudley's tea.'

'Oh dear! Did I? Did I *really*? What about you, then? You almost had me killed! Call yourself a friend?'

'What are you complaining about? I saved you, didn't I?'

'Yes, when I was just about on the ground!'

'I keep telling you, I only remembered the spell

at the last minute. Wish I hadn't remembered it at all now. Here.' Sharkadder threw *The Daily Miracle* at Pongwiffy. 'Look for yourself. I'm tired of doing all the work.'

Pongwiffy, without looking, declared that she didn't like the sound of any of them. Sharkadder pointed out that beggars couldn't be choosers. Pongwiffy said that her arm still hurt and she couldn't be bothered. Sharkadder remarked that she had better be bothered.

'Because . . .' she said spitefully. 'Because you're not staying with me any longer.'

Pongwiffy scowled. Things were heading for a crisis. She picked at her piece of dry bread and hummed mournfully to herself. Sharkadder finished her breakfast in silence, cleared away, painted her face, put on her hat and went out shopping. When she came back, Pongwiffy was slumped in the same position, looking forlorn and pulling threads from her sling.

Sharkadder cooked lunch and ate the lot in full view of Pongwiffy, who looked even sadder. Finally, Sharkadder could bear it no longer.

'All right!' she screamed. 'All right! I'll come with you, just this once! Anything to get rid of you.

But I claim the right to break friends first thing tomorrow morning. And that's when you go, Pongwiffy, whether you've found a house or not. Agreed?'

'Agreed,' said Pongwiffy sniffily. 'Never liked you much anyway.'

They had an awful day. They tried every single place that *The Daily Miracle* had to offer. They saw warrens, lairs and holes in the ground. They trailed through caverns, caves and cowsheds. They inspected a log cabin, a caravan and even a wigwam. They trooped tiredly around sheds, shacks and shanties. None of them, for one reason or another, was quite right. In desperation, Pongwiffy even agreed to look over the pretty little cottage with the lovely views. It was every bit as charming as the advertisement said it was. Pongwiffy loathed it.

The moon was beginning to rise as they wended their way back to Sharkadder's place. They were quarrelling loudly.

'I've never known such a fusspot,' Sharkadder yelled.

'Well, I'm sorry, but I didn't like any of them,'

33

Pongwiffy yelled back.

'Well, don't blame me when you're homeless tomorrow.'

'Certainly I shall blame you. How you could throw out a homeless friend with a bad arm, I just don't know.'

'I'm not throwing a friend out. I'm throwing *you* out.'

'I thought we weren't breaking friends till tomorrow,' muttered Pongwiffy.

'That's when I'm throwing you out!'

'How you could throw out a homeless friend with a bad arm, I just don't know . . .'

And so on.

Suddenly, Pongwiffy stopped and sniffed. Sharkadder continued marching on in a very bad temper indeed.

'Just a minute, Sharky,' hissed Pongwiffy, nose twitching. 'That smell! That beautiful smell. What is it?'

'Smells like a rubbish tip,' answered Sharkadder, trying not to breathe too deeply.

'That's it! That's exactly what it is! I was brought up on one of those, you know. Oooh, that smell . . . reminds me of my childhood. Do you think we could take a little look?'

'What, NOW?'

'Please, Sharky. It would mean so much to me. Oh, please.'

'Oh – bother! Come *on* then, if you must,' said Sharkadder with a sigh.

Together they followed their noses to the source of the smell. It wasn't far away.

'What a sight!' whispered Pongwiffy, awestruck. 'A rubbish tip under the moon. Brings tears to the eyes.'

'Hmm. Very nice.' Sharkadder was fidgeting, wanting to get back home to Dudley.

'What's that over there?' Pongwiffy pointed. 'There, look. No, *there*, idiot. Behind that pile of old mattresses. Left of the broken pram. Near the rusty cooker. Surely you can see. Look, over by the cat food tins. Right of that old carpet! There, see it? *There!*'

Sharkadder squinted. 'What, that? You mean that broken-down old hovel?'

But Pongwiffy was off, running like the wind, as fast as her legs would carry her. When Sharkadder caught up with her, she was standing in the doorway of the broken-down old hovel.

The door was open – or, to be exact, it was lying amongst the weeds in a sea of flaking paint, having finally parted company with its rusty hinges. Broken windows sagged in their frames, and the roof was full of holes. A dreadful smell of damp and decay wafted from the dark interior. Pongwiffy was inhaling the stench, eyes closed in ecstasy.

'What *are* you playing at, Pong?' snapped Sharkadder crossly. 'What's so special about an empty, smelly old hovel?'

Pongwiffy's eyes opened and she smiled and blinked as though coming round from a trance.

'Sharky,' she said, with a happy grin. 'Sharky, my old friend. This is it. The end of the line. I've found it. Welcome to my new home.'

CHAPTER THREE
The Over-Familiar Familiar

'Well? How are you settling in?' asked Sharkadder a few days later. Pongwiffy had popped in to borrow Sharkadder's spare cauldron. Her own, of course, was dented beyond repair. She was hanging around in the hope that Sharkadder might offer some breakfast.

'Wonderfully,' said Pongwiffy. 'I've nearly finished. I've fixed the door. I managed to rescue lots of stuff from the cave. It's lucky my Wand's better. I'd never have been able to lift all those boulders by myself. Of course, I didn't bother with some of it. It helps being next to the rubbish tip. I found all my furniture there, you know.'

Strangely enough, although she tried to speak cheerfully, she sounded a bit glum.

'I hope you've cleaned it up a bit,' remarked Sharkadder, who was sitting at a cracked mirror, gently warming her set of hedgehog hair rollers over a candle. Lipsticks and little bottles of nail varnish in hideous shades littered the table.

'Clean it? Whatever for? It's just perfect the way it is,' said Pongwiffy. 'Why don't you come and see this afternoon?'

'Too busy,' said Sharkadder. 'Dudley and I are working on a new spell.'

'Oh,' said Pongwiffy, disappointed. 'Oh. Another time, then.' And she gave a little sigh.

'What's the matter, Pong?' asked Sharkadder, seeing her friend's crestfallen face. 'I thought you loved your new hovel.'

'Oh, I do, I do. It's just . . . well, to be honest, Sharky, I'm feeling a bit lonely. It's very quiet at the rubbish tip. I haven't seen a soul in the last three days.'

'Hmm. You know what you need,' said Sharkadder, diving after a cross, overheated hedgehog who had plopped from the table and was desperately making for the door. 'You need a Familiar. You're the only Witch I know who hasn't got one.'

'I've got my flies,' said Pongwiffy, pointing. Buzz and Dave came zooming back from the biscuit tin and circled loyally around the point of her tall hat.

'Flies? Flies don't count.'

Buzz and Dave buzzed angrily. But she was right. Flies don't count. A Familiar, according to the dictionary, is: *a demon attending and obeying a Witch*. Familiars, however, don't have to be demons. They can be cats, owls, crows, bats – anything you like, really, as long as they've got a bit of intelligence. That puts the likes of Buzz and Dave right out of the running. There's so much to pack into a fly's small body, there's just no room for intelligence.

'Apart from anything else, think of the time you'd save,' continued Sharkadder. 'Don't you get tired of running your own messages and collecting your own ingredients? Not to mention doing all your own spying.'

Pongwiffy had to confess that she did.

'There you are then! Stuck in that old hovel with only your Broom for company. No wonder you're fed up. You definitely need a Familiar. All the best Witches have them. I don't know what I'd do without darling Dudley. Put the kettle on, and we'll write an advertisement over a nice cup of hot bogwater. You can put it in *The Daily Miracle.*'

Pongwiffy filled the kettle carefully. Sharkadder's darling was perched on the draining board next to the sink, crooning a sea shanty whilst sharpening his teeth with a file.

'We pushed him off the plank, miaow,
We clapped him when he sank, miaow,
Oh what a jolly prank, miaow,
When Filthy Frank was drowned-O!'

sang Dudley in a tuneless dirge.

'What a pretty tune, Dudley,' said Sharkadder. 'I do love it when you sing.'

Pongwiffy accidentally sprinkled three drops of water on the tip of Dudley's tail. Only three little drops, that's all, but you should have heard him!

'Ye cack-handed, clumsy old crow, I'll hang ye from the yardarm! I'll have ye pulverised and thrown to the fishes, be danged if I don't!'

'He likes you really,' said Sharkadder, rolling up the last hedgehog. 'That's just his way of speaking.' She took a bottle marked *Old Sock* and dabbed some behind her ears. 'Want some?'

'No,' said Pongwiffy proudly. 'I have my own built-in smell.' True. Compared to Pongwiffy, *Old Sock* smelt like a garden of roses.

'Now, we need a paper and pencil, then we must put on our Thinking Caps.' Sharkadder bustled about in a businesslike way.

'I haven't brought mine,' said Pongwiffy.

'Never mind, we'll take turns with mine. Come to mother, Dudley, and sit on my lap.'

Dudley stretched, yawned and thumped heavily on to Sharkadder's sharp knees. He rubbed himself against her chin, purring loudly.

'Isn't he sweet? Isn't he a darling? He's my Dudley. My cuddly-wuddly Dudley,' cooed Sharkadder adoringly, picking hairs off her lipstick. 'Of course, you'll never find a Familiar like Dudley, Pong. Not many Witches are so lucky.'

'No,' agreed Pongwiffy, hoping that her bad luck would hold. She certainly didn't want a Familiar like Dudley.

All that day they worked on the advertisement. The floor was a sea of screwed-up pieces of paper and broken pencils before they got it just right. Even the Thinking Cap was fit for nothing, and had to be thrown away.

'It's rather good, isn't it?' said Pongwiffy many hours later, peering with red, bleary eyes at the finished product.

'It's brilliant,' agreed Sharkadder, who had done most of the work. 'Read it again. I could listen to it all night.'

**'WANTED – FAMILIAR,
apply to Witch Pongwiffy, The Hovel
Number One, Dump Edge,
Witchway Wood.
No time-wasters.'**

Sharkadder stood up and began taking the hedgehogs from her hair. She placed them tidily in a little box, where they lay in rows, still snoring.

'I'm sure that'll do the trick, Pong. Good job you had me to help you.'

'It was,' said Pongwiffy gratefully. 'Thanks, Sharky. Thanks for the meals too. You're a good friend.' And off she went to the postbox.

By the following night, Pongwiffy had forgotten all about her advertisement. She was too busy preparing her supper to think about anything else. Her supper was giving her problems. It was Toad-in-the-Hole. She had made the Hole – a nice deep one in the lumpy grey batter. The trouble lay in getting the Toad to stay in it. Every time she turned her back to reach for the salt, its head would pop out again, a tetchy expression on its face.

'I've told you a hundred times. Get back down and *stay* down,' snapped Pongwiffy, puffing up the fire with the bellows.

'Why?' complained the Toad, who liked explanations.

'Because you're my supper, that's why! Now, get back in that Hole!'

'Shan't,' sulked the Toad.

Pongwiffy whacked it smartly on the head with a spoon. The Toad submerged, muttering vague threats.

'Now then, what next? Ah yes. Lay the table.'

Laying the table wasn't as easy as it sounds.

Tottering towers of dirty dishes reached almost to the rafters. They had been growing steadily taller all week, for Pongwiffy, being a Witch of Dirty Habits, couldn't be bothered to clear them away. Some had green mould on them, the ones at the top were festooned with cobwebs, and a family of cockroaches had set up house in one of the teacups.

'Oh well,' said Pongwiffy with a frown. 'Suppose I'll just have to deal with these dishes.'

She stretched out a finger, and gave the nearest tower a little push. It teetered for a moment, then toppled slowly, crashing to the floor in a nasty mess of broken china and mouldy leftovers. Pongwiffy collapsed into the nearest chair, exhausted. She wasn't used to housework.

That was when the doorbell rang.

'Oh – botheration! Who's that?'

Hastily she glanced at her reflection in a bent teapot, and rubbed a bit of dirt into her nose. The doorbell continued to ring with an insistent, irritating, teeth-on-edge jangling.

'Answer it! Answer it!' begged the Toad, who had a bad headache. Unable to bear the racket, it plunged back into the batter and tried to relax.

'All right, all right!' snarled Pongwiffy, hurrying

to the door and snatching it open.

First she thought there was no one there. Then she saw it. A small, cute, honey-coloured Hamster with pink paws was dangling by its teeth from her bell-rope. As it swung from side to side, the cracked bell continued to jangle harshly inside the hovel.

'Here – hang on a minute! Get *down* from there!' ordered Pongwiffy severely.

'Vat I do?' asked the Hamster with difficulty, speaking between clenched teeth. ' 'Ang on or get down?'

'Get *down*!'

The Hamster dropped down, light as a leaf, nose twitching.

'Coo! Vat a pong! You are Pongviffy. Ya, I come to ze right place.' And the Hamster scuttled past her into the hovel, leaving a trail of minute paw marks in the thick dust coating the floor.

What a cheek! Pongwiffy was speechless.

'Is big tip in 'ere,' remarked the Hamster, staring around. 'Don't you not never do no 'ousework?'

'Big *tip*? How dare you!' said Pongwiffy, finding her voice at last. 'I don't know who you think you are, but I want you out of my hovel this minute.'

' 'Ugo,' said the Hamster, still looking around.

45

'I *beg* your pardon? *Me* go?' Pongwiffy couldn't believe her ears.

'No, no! Is name. 'Ugo. Viz an H.'

'Well, look here, Hugo-with-an-H, I don't know what you want, but . . .'

'I vant ze job.'

'Job? What job?'

'Vitch Familiar. I see advert in paper. I come for interview. So. Interview me.'

And Hugo-with-an-H climbed up the table leg and settled himself comfortably against the bent teapot, paws folded in his lap.

'I shall do no such thing. You're not suitable. Goodbye.'

''Ow you know zat till you interview me?' asked Hugo reasonably.

'I can tell. We Witches know these things. You're just not the right type. Traditionally speaking.'

'Vat is right type?' Hugo had found a pile of crumbs, and was busily stuffing them into his cheek pouches.

'Well – cats, of course. Weasels, ferrets, stoats – that sort of thing. Bats. Crows. Toads occasionally, if you can find an intelligent one.' Pongwiffy glared spite-fully at the Toad-in-the-Hole, who had its

46

head stuck out as usual and was listening with interest to the conversation.

'The thing is,' she continued, 'the *main* thing is, a good Familiar has to be ugly or wicked, or better still, both. A good Familiar is *never* cute and fluffy. With a silly accent.'

'Meanink me?' enquired Hugo. He spoke mildly, but there was a dangerous glint in his eye.

'Most certainly. Just look at yourself. You're sweet and cuddly. To a disgusting degree, actually. But then, you're a Hamster. You lot are supposed to be cute. Nice, gentle little things who live in cages and get tickled under the chin, like this . . .'

Pongwiffy stretched out a bony finger, then snatched it back hastily, unprepared for the sudden transformation. Hugo had shot to his feet, back arched and fur bristling. His lips were curled back in a snarl, exposing rows of wicked-looking little teeth, and a deep growl rumbled and throbbed in his small throat. If he had had a tail to speak of, it would have lashed. He didn't, so instead he lashed his whiskers. He was indeed an awesome sight.

Pongwiffy eyed him uneasily. After a moment, he gave a little shake, his fur flattened, his whiskers subsided, and he sat down and scratched his left ear with his right hind leg. Pongwiffy wondered if she had imagined it.

'You 'ave sumpsink to eat?' he asked. 'Little bit of carrot? Apple, maybe? I come a long way from 'ome.'

'No,' said Pongwiffy. 'Go away. The interview's over.'

''Ow can zis be? You 'ave not asked me questions.'

Pongwiffy sighed. It was getting late, and she still hadn't had her supper. This pushy Hamster was beginning to get on her nerves.

'Now listen,' she snapped. 'Put yourself in my place – er . . .'

''Ugo. Viz an H.'

'Yes, yes, whatever your silly name is. Now, how do you think it would look if I turned up at the next meeting with you in tow? I'd die of embarrassment. All the others will be there with their Familiars . . .'

'Uzzers? Vat uzzers?'

'The other Witches in the Coven. Thirteen of us, including me. That's the right number for a Coven, you know.'

'Tell me about zem,' said Hugo, sounding interested.

'Well, there's Grandwitch Sourmuddle, of course – she's Mistress of the Coven. Her Familiar's a Demon, name of Snoop. Then there's Sharkadder, my best friend – she's got Dead Eye Dudley. Cats are always popular as Familiars. Agglebag and Bagaggle – that's the twins – they've got Cats too, Siamese ones, IdentiKit and CopiCat. Witch Macabre – she's got that hideous Haggis creature, Rory. Bendyshanks, now, she's got a Snake, and Gaga – well, she's Bats, of course. Sludgegooey's got this Fiend called Filth – he plays the drums, you know. Then there's Bonidle – she's got a Sloth. Scrofula's got a Vulture, Greymatter's got an Owl, and Ratsnappy's got a Rat. I think that's everybody.'

'Except you. You 'ave nussink.'

'Yes, and I'd sooner have nussink than a Hamster, thanks very much. The very idea!'

'Ah. But me, I not just any 'amster.'

'All Hamsters are the same to me, kiddo. Now off you go, there's a good little chap. You've wasted enough of my time. Run away and be somebody's pet.'

'*Eeeeeeaaaaaooooerrgr!*'

A piercing scream of anguish shattered the peace of the night. Twirling around on the spot, Pongwiffy clamped her hand to her left earlobe, which had developed a sharp, agonising pain. It was the sort of pain you might get if a small Hamster was attached by its teeth to your ear. That sort of pain.

'Ah, ah, ah, ah, ah!' gasped Pongwiffy in breathless little screams, hopping on the spot and flapping vainly at the small dangling bundle of fur just outside her vision. 'Ah, ah, AH! LEGGO! GERROFF! GERROFF!'

Hugo hung on.

'LEGGO, I say! LET GO, OR I'LL PUT YOU THROUGH THE MINCER! I WILL, I'M WARNING YOUUUUUUUU . . .'

Hugo hung on.

'DO YOU WANT TO BE A HAMSTER-BURGER? DO YOU? AH, AH, AH, AH!' Pongwiffy danced around, braying piteously through gritted teeth.

Hugo hung on.

'Please!' whimpered Pongwiffy, changing tack, begging now. 'Let go and I'll give you crumbs! Hundreds of 'em. I'll give you an apple core, promise! PROMISE!'

Hugo hung on.

Pongwiffy danced around the room a bit more.

50

The Toad-in-the-Hole clapped, enjoying her performance.

'I'LL PUT A SPELL ON YOU! I WILL! JUST YOU WAIT!' raged Pongwiffy, and searched her brains for a spell to dislodge Hamsters from earlobes. The search was in vain. Her brain was empty of all but one word. The word said PAIN.

'What is it you want? What? WHAT?' snivelled Pongwiffy with tears in her eyes.

'Trial,' said Hugo, as distinctly as he could through a mouthful of earlobe. 'Proper trial. Zen you decide if I goot or not.'

'All right, all *right*! You've got it! Pax! I give in.'

To her intense relief, Hugo's jaws unclenched and he plopped lightly on to her shoulder.

'So sorry,' he said politely, then scuttled down her arm and jumped to the floor where he nosed about looking for more crumbs.

Pongwiffy leapt to the sink and began dabbing at her smarting ear with a dirty rag. Her cheeks were flushed with the shame of it. She was glad there had been no witnesses. She wouldn't like it spread about that Pongwiffy had been attacked by a crazed Hamster. She didn't count the Toad. She should have. He gossiped it about something shocking when he recovered from his ordeal some time later.

Meanwhile, Hugo went snuffling about beneath the piles of broken crockery, stuffing his pouches with any food he could find.

The Toad took advantage of the situation, escaping through a crack in the door and hopping off into the night, leaving small puddles of batter.

'Blackmail. Blackmailed by a Hamster!' snarled Pongwiffy, dabbing at the teeth marks.

'Ya,' agreed Hugo cheerfully, emerging from beneath a cracked plate with a blackened toast crust in his paw. 'But is your own fault. You say zat vord I no like.'

'What word?'

'Pet. 'Ugo is not Pet. Let me tell you sumsink.' Hugo settled himself comfortably on the rug in front of the fire and gnawed at the toast as he talked.

'Vere I come from, all ze 'amsters is pets. Ze 'ole of mine family become ze pets. Bruzzers, sisters, muzzer, fazzer – pets, pets, all of zem pets. Is disgrace. Make me mad.'

'Where do you come from?' asked Pongwiffy curiously.

' 'Amsterdam. Vere you sink? Anyvay, all my family are livink in ze cage, running around on ze

53

stupid veel all day. Vat a life! Sometimes get taken out for cuddle. Not me. Zey try to cuddle me, zey get bite, no problem. I not pet material.'

'You can say that again,' muttered Pongwiffy, searching for a tube of Instant Cure-All.

'So, I make plans,' continued Hugo. 'I vork on ze muscles – plenty nuts, press-ups, vork-outs on ze veel, you know. Zen, von night, I am strong. Bend back bars and set out to seek ze fortune. I 'ave many adventures. You vant to 'ear?'

'No,' said Pongwiffy sulkily, still rummaging. 'I am in great pain.'

'Is goot story. You vill like. Ze Champion 'Amster escapes from ze cage to fight for ze Great Cause.'

'What Great Cause?'

''Amsters Are Angry.'

'Are they? I can't say I've noticed.'

'Zey vill be. Soon as zey 'ear about ze missed job opportunities.'

'What job opportunities?'

'Vitch Familiar.'

'Now, look. About that . . .'

'Look, I vant no arguments, OK? I 'ave – ow you say – set my 'eart on it. Trial is agreed. Tell me about ze job.'

Pongwiffy sighed. She had just noticed that her supper was missing its vital ingredient, her ear hurt, the Instant Cure-All was missing and she was too tired to argue any more.

'Oh – all right. If I must. Well, you'll have to help me with my spells, of course. And run messages. Bit of spying, that sort of thing. Telling on people.'

'Vonderful!' said Hugo enthusiastically. ' 'Ugo like to squeal.'

'But I'm only trying you out, mind. And you'll have to do exactly as I say. You're not at all what I had in mind, you know.'

'You not 'ave big choice. I ze only applicant, ya?'

'Ah,' replied Pongwiffy. 'But I expect loads will turn up tomorrow.'

'Zat I doubt,' said Hugo. 'You are most smelly, if you don't mind my mentionink it.'

'Not at all. Thanks,' said Pongwiffy, flattered.

'Vat I call you? Pong?'

'Certainly not. That's much too over-familiar for a Familiar. You're not much more than a servant really, you know. You must call me O Mistress.'

'OK,' agreed Hugo cheerfully. 'Now. Vere I am goink to sleep, O Mistress?'

'How should I know? Somewhere where I'll step

on you when I get out of bed tomorrow morning,'
said Pongwiffy spitefully.

Secretly, though, she rather liked being called O
Mistress. It had a certain ring to it.

CHAPTER FOUR
The Trial

Hugo's Trial was, to Pongwiffy's surprise, not as big a trial as she thought it was going to be. He made himself useful in a dozen different ways, and didn't take up much room. He took to Magic like a duck takes to water, having a good nose for where to find the right ingredients and shouting encouraging, admiring things like, 'Ya! Zat vas a corker, zat vas!' when Pongwiffy conjured up pink explosions in the air or turned herself into a jar of Marmite. He was thrilled with the simplest spells, and Making Magic was more fun, somehow, when he was around.

Pongwiffy found herself beginning to enjoy his company in the evenings. He was a born storyteller – some might say fibber – and would entertain her for hours with his tales of *Ze Escape From Ze Cage, Ze Fight Viz Ze Mountain Lion, Ze Voyage Around Ze Cape of Death*, and so on. In fact, by the end of the week, she had grown quite attached to him and found herself thinking that Hamsters made rather good Familiars, if Hugo was anything to go by.

However, there was one very big problem. How was she going to explain him to the other Witches? Imagine confessing to having a Hamster as a Familiar! It didn't bear thinking about.

She rather hoped that Hugo wouldn't insist on coming to the monthly Meeting which was to be held next Friday night on Crag Hill. She worried about it all week, then came up with a plan. The plan was to Sneak Out Very Quietly. It might have worked too, except that Hugo sneaked first. He had crept into her hat, rightly suspecting foul play. He was so small and light that Pongwiffy didn't even feel him sitting on her head.

Congratulating herself, she mounted her Broom and rode through the night, chuckling as she thought of Hugo curled up fast asleep in the tea cosy he used for a bed. She could stop worrying about the problem for another month. By then, maybe she would have thought of something.

After a long, chilly ride, Crag Hill loomed before her. Pongwiffy zoomed in and left her Broom gossiping with the others in the Broom park.

'Ve 'ave touch down?' demanded a familiar voice, close to her ear. 'Vat 'appens now?'

Pongwiffy nearly collapsed with the shock. She snatched off her tall hat and peered into the gloomy depths. Hugo's beady little eyes gazed up, full of excitement.

'Who said you could come?' she hissed furiously. 'Did I say you could come? Did I? Did I say . . .'

'Yoo-hoo! Is that you, Pong?' That was Sharkadder.

Pongwiffy hastily rammed her hat back on.

'Stay in there and keep quiet,' she snapped. 'Or else!'

'Ven I get introduced?'

'Never. Later. Maybe. We'll see. Now SHHHH.' To her relief, Hugo shushed. Pongwiffy walked through the trees and went to join Sharkadder, who was roasting beetles in the embers of a merrily blazing bonfire.

Nearby, the Witches Sludgegooey and Bendyshanks were busily making sandwiches and setting them out on trestle tables. There was a choice of three fillings – spiderspread, frog paste, or fleas and pickle. Gaga, as usual, was hanging upside-down from a tree with her Bats, who lined the branches like rows of old black socks. Scrofula and Ratsnappy were swapping knitting patterns, Bonidle was asleep, and Greymatter was composing a poem and sipping thoughtfully from a glass of dirty pondwater. That only left Grandwitch Sourmuddle, Agglebag and Bagaggle, and Macabre to be accounted for – but they were always the last to arrive.

Elsewhere, the Familiars were chatting in little groups. Scrofula's Vulture was talking about a personal problem to Filth the Fiend, who was tapping out drum rhythms on a tree stump with his eyes closed, not really paying attention. Bonidle's Sloth was slumped in a pile of leaves, snoring every bit as loudly as his mistress. He didn't have a name – Bonidle couldn't be bothered to give him one – and the Sloth was too apathetic to even care.

Slithering Steve, a small grass snake and Bendyshanks' Familiar, was moonbathing on

60

a rock, pretending not to care that he wasn't poisonous. Greymatter's Owl, whose name was Speks and who was intelligent, was talking to Ratsnappy's Rat, whose name was Vernon and who wasn't. He was good at mazes, though.

'Hello, Pong. Have a beetle,' said Sharkadder gaily. She was dressed up to the nines in her smartest rags. She was wearing her greenest lipstick and her longest spiderleg false eyelashes. Squiggly strands of greasy hair hung like potato peelings down her back. She had evidently been at the hedgehogs again.

Dead Eye Dudley lounged at her feet, flicking his tail and giving everyone dirty looks out of his single yellow eye. He spat rudely as Pongwiffy approached, then wandered off to strike fear into the hearts of his fellow Familiars, who buttered him up and called him Cap'n.

'Now then, Pong,' said Sharkadder. 'Tell me. Did you get a lot of replies to our advertisement?'

'Er ... well, not a *lot*,' said Pongwiffy uncomfortably. 'Actually.'

'How many?' pressed Sharkadder.

'One,' said Pongwiffy. 'Actually.' She felt Hugo stir eagerly under her hat.

'Well? Did you hire it?'

61

'No,' said Pongwiffy, and came out in green spots. This always happened when she told fibs. Just as well, or she'd tell them all the time.

'Well – it's sort of on trial. Actually,' she amended hastily, and the spots died down.

'Did you bring it with you?'

'No. OUCH!' The green spots reappeared, and Pongwiffy did an odd little hop as Hugo gave her a warning nip. 'I mean yes.'

Sharkadder stared curiously, and Pongwiffy pretended she was trying out a new dance step.

'Well, where is it, then?' snapped Sharkadder. 'What's the big secret? Is it a ferret or a weasel or what? Is it over by the Brooms?' She was peering around curiously, hoping to spot an unfamiliar Familiar.

'Now?' whispered Hugo.

'What was that?' demanded Sharkadder suspiciously. 'A squeak came from under your hat.'

'Oh *really*?' said Pongwiffy with a casual yawn. 'Actually, I think you must be mistaken, Sharky. Look, you've still got a hedgehog roller in. It must have been that.'

'It was nothing of the sort! You've got something under there, Pongwiffy, and if it's your new Familiar you might at least be polite enough to introduce me. Seeing as I did the advertisement for you.' Sharkadder stamped her foot crossly.

'Well – all right, Sharky, I do have something under there,' confessed Pongwiffy. 'But I'd sooner keep it under my hat for now, ha ha.'

'Why?' persisted Sharkadder.

'Er – too terrifying. It'll scare you.' Back came the green spots.

'Nonsense! You're lying to me, Pongwiffy, I can tell. In fact, there's this rumour going round, you know. Dudley heard it from a Toad . . .'

'Oh look! There's old – er – you know. Must have a word with her!' cried Pongwiffy, and scuttled off.

'I'll break friends!' shouted Sharkadder after her. Pongwiffy pretended not to hear, and made for the trestle tables. She snatched a sandwich and popped it under her hat for Hugo. Eating was the only thing that kept him quiet.

'You're not supposed to start on them yet,' said Bendyshanks in a bossy voice. 'Not till Grandwitch Sourmuddle arrives. You know The Rules. And why did you put it under your hat?'

'Mind your own business,' said Pongwiffy rudely. 'What would you rather I did? Pushed it up your nose?'

Now, that is just the sort of rude comment that is sure to start an argument – so it was just as well that at that very moment, there was an interruption. A terrible squawling noise rent the air. Imagine a hundred cats all having their tails pulled at the same time. It was rather like that, but worse.

'Jumpink gerbils!' exclaimed Hugo in his dark, stuffy cone. 'Vat in ze vorld is 'appenink?'

'Sssh! Stop scrabbling! It's Grandwitch Sourmuddle.' And Pongwiffy stood to attention, along with everyone else.

From out of the pine trees came a small procession. First came Agglebag and Bagaggle, the identical twins, playing their violins. The noise they made was a cross between a dentist's drill and a cow with severe stomach-ache. IdentiKit and CopiCat twined identically in and out of their legs.

Behind them came Witch Macabre in her ceremonial tartan rags. She was riding on her Haggis – an odd-looking creature called Rory with a great deal of shaggy fur and a daft ginger fringe which hung down over its eyes, causing it to trip up every third or fourth step. To add to the racket, Witch Macabre was playing her bagpipes, breaking off every so often to shout, 'Oot o' the way, ye Sassenachs! Make way foor Wee Grandwitch Sourmuddle, Mistress o' the Coven!'

Grandwitch Sourmuddle tottered along vaguely at the rear, wondering what she was doing there. She was so old, she tended to forget things. On her shoulder sat Snoop, her demon Familiar, looking bored.

The procession came to a halt before the bonfire. Agglebag and Bagaggle played their final ear-splitting chord with a flourish, and the drone of the bagpipes wheezed to a halt. There was a general sigh of relief, and everyone waited respectfully for the Grandwitch to speak her important first words.

'Where am I?' she said. Snoop whispered in her ear.

'Yes, yes, I can see *that*, Snoop. I can see I'm on Crag Hill. But what's the occasion? My birthday or something? Where's the cake?'

'It's the monthly Meeting, Grandwitch. You're supposed to do your speech,' Snoop reminded her, as he always did.

'Speech, you say? What, before I blow out the candles?'

'There are no candles. There is no cake. Just the usual Meeting,' said Snoop patiently.

'They could have made me a cake. Mean old hags,' whined Sourmuddle.

'It's not your birthday. Just the usual Meeting.'

The assembled throng yawned and shuffled, rather hoping Grandwitch Sourmuddle would retire soon.

'Do your speech. Then we can have the sandwiches,' suggested Snoop.

'Sandwiches? That's all there ever is, stale old sandwiches. Oh well, better get started I suppose. Hail, Witches!'

'Hail!' came the response, and as always a small cloud came hurtling through the night sky and delivered a short, sharp burst of hailstones before scuttling off again in a northerly direction.

'I declare this supermarket open,' announced Sourmuddle, digging hailstones out of her ears. There was an uncertain pause while Snoop whispered again, making impatient gestures with his small, green, webbed hands.

'Sorry. Meeting. I declare this Meeting open.'

'Hooray!' shouted the Witches, and fell upon the sandwiches. Snoop tutted and spoke urgently into

Sourmuddle's ear.

'Oh. Right. HOLD IT!'

Agglebag and Bagaggle played a single, important-sounding discord on their violins, and Witch Macabre raised her bagpipes threateningly to her lips. The Haggis blew the fringe out of his eyes and gave a warning cough. Everyone stood stock still, sandwiches half in and half out of mouths.

'News-time first,' ordered Sourmuddle. 'Then I cut the cake. Now, has anyone got any news we should all hear? Any new spells? Anyone done anything particularly horrible to a Goblin? No? Right then, in that case . . .'

'Wait!' Sharkadder pointed an accusing finger at Pongwiffy, who guessed what was coming and cringed.

'Pongwiffy's got some news!' announced Sharkadder in a clear, firm voice. 'She's hired a new Familiar.'

Everyone turned and looked at Pongwiffy. The Familiars rustled and flapped and looked expectant.

'Eh? Oh. Well, come on then, Pongwiffy, but make it snappy. I want to open my birthday presents. Up to the fire.'

Wishing the ground would open up and

swallow her, Pongwiffy slowly walked towards the fire, which is where you have to stand if you have news to tell. Under her hat, Hugo busily attended to his whiskers and brushed the crumbs from his chin. He wanted to look smart for his first appearance.

'Go on, Pong!' called Sharkadder in a mean sort of way. 'Don't be shy. Introduce us to your Familiar.'

Twelve white bony faces stared at Pongwiffy expectantly.

'She says it's terrifying. That's all she'd tell me. Although I used to be her best friend and even wrote the advertisement for her,' Sharkadder told the assembled company.

'Hurry up, Pong, we're all waiting!' clamoured the audience.

For a brief moment, Pongwiffy considered saying a quick spell which would transform Hugo into a wolf or a lizard, anything that wasn't cute – but Witches aren't so easily deceived, and she knew that she'd never get away with it. She gulped and took a deep breath.

'Actually . . .' she said. 'Actually, he's a bit shy.'

'Show us! Show us! Show us your Familiar!' came the chant, and Sharkadder started a slow handclap.

'I'd sooner not introduce him right now, if you

don't mind . . .'

'Boo! Against The Rules!' Which it was. Witches have the right to know about each other's Familiars. That way, no one has an unfair advantage.

It was no good. Pongwiffy knew that her hour of doom was at hand. Better to get the whole embarrassing thing over and done with.

'All right!' she said sulkily. 'If you must know, he's under my hat. And he's a . . . he's a . . . actually, he's a Hamster.'

There was a terrible, sickening pause which seemed to go on for ever. Then – which was worse – The Laughter began. It started as titters. Little sniggers and snickers, and the odd tee-hee. Then came chuckles and chortles, followed closely by hoots and guffaws. The Witches cackled, cawed, jeered, scoffed, shrieked, bellowed, howled and gibbered. Witches hung on to each other for support. Witches banged their heads against nearby trees. Witches pointed shaking fingers at Pongwiffy, then collapsed to the ground, clutching their sides and gasping for breath.

Oh, the shame of it!

Pongwiffy hung her head as the waves of derision rolled over her. She would never live it down. She would have to move hovel and go far, far away where nobody knew her.

And under her hat, Hugo's eyes began to turn red.

'A Hamster! Oh, I can't bear it!' howled Bendyshanks, rolling around in the leaves and kicking her legs in the air.

'Where is he? Show us your Hamster, Pongwiffy! Terrify us!' begged Sludgegooey.

The Familiars were exchanging superior sideways glances with each other. They wanted to laugh too, but were used to taking their cue from Dudley. And Dudley wasn't laughing. Dudley was sneering. His single yellow eye blazed and his crooked tail whipped from side to side. Menacingly, he swaggered forward, muscles rippling.

'Well now, boys,' he drawled. 'An 'amster, be it? An 'amster seekin' to join the crew? What'll it be next? I asks meself. A Christmas tree fairy?'

The Familiars fell about laughing. Dudley raised a paw, and there was instant silence.

'Let's be havin' a look at this 'ere 'amster,' continued Dudley. 'Let's see what we'm up against. Must admit to bein' curious. Seems to me Witch Familiar bain't a suitable job for an 'amster. Weak,

70

fluffy little things as a rule.'

Crouched in the darkness of Pongwiffy's hat, Hugo was beside himself. How *dare* they laugh at him! And as for the owner of that sneering voice – just let him wait! Blind with rage, he threw himself at the walls of the hat, tearing at the lining with his sharp little teeth.

'Not a suitable job at all,' came Dudley's hateful hiss again. 'Seems to me this 'ere 'amster's got delusions of grandeur, lads, what say you? A kiddy's pet, that's more like what an 'amster should be.'

That did it. From beneath Pongwiffy's hat came a shrill squeal of outrage. Both Witches and Familiars took an involuntary step back, their mouths dropping open. Pongwiffy snatched off her tall hat and revealed what looked at first sight to be a maddened nail brush on top of her head.

'This is Hugo,' announced Pongwiffy. 'He's from Hamsterdam. And he doesn't like being called a pet, Dudley. Not one little bit.'

Hugo descended in three easy steps – head to shoulder, shoulder to hand, hand to ground. He landed right next to Dudley's nose. The firelight reflected red in his eyes. His whiskers were seething, his teeth were gnashing, his ears were flattened, his back was arched, his fur was standing on end. Cute, he wasn't. Even Pongwiffy edged away from him.

Dudley, however, that tough, battle-scarred veteran, stood his ground. Slowly he licked his lips and smiled a thin, cold cat smile.

'Say zat again!' raged Hugo. 'Say zat again, you old bag of vind. Who you sink you is? I tell you vat you is. A bus for ze fleas, zat's vat! I see zem 'opping on and off from 'ere!'

A gasp went up from Witches and Familiars alike. Nobody ever spoke that way to Dudley.

'Well, well,' scoffed Dudley. 'So it's mutiny, eh? Lookin' for trouble, are ye, little feller? Wantin' ter challenge the Cap'n. Well, I ought ter teach yer a lesson, I s'pose, but 'tain't right. You'm just too small. I bain't that much of a bully. I expect yer mummy'll put you on the naughty step, save me the trouble. Go play on yer wheel, sonny. Off with ye, before I change me mind. Go and be some little kid's pet.' And with a sneer, Dudley turned his back and prepared to swagger away.

Meeeeeeaaaaaoooeeeeergr!'

We all recognise that, don't we? It's almost exactly the same as that blood-curdling howl invented by Pongwiffy when Hugo did his earring impression.

Perhaps a little different. This time, Hugo had opted for the tail.

Dudley whirled round, shaking his head in pain and astonishment. Of course, the source of the agony was still behind him. He tried lashing his tail to shake Hugo off. Hugo merely bit harder. Dudley skittered backwards, wriggling his rear end and roaring such dreadful piratical curses that even the Witches were shocked.

'Terrific, isn't he?' said Pongwiffy proudly to Sharkadder, who was rooted to the spot, frozen with horror as she watched the contortions of her darling.

'Get off! Get *off me tail*, ye pint-sized pompom off a pirate's bobble hat! I'll trim yer sails! I'll run ye aground! I'll scupper ye, rot me for a ship's biscuit else! I'll mangle ye with me binnacle! Meeeahhhhh!'

Hugo hung on.

'Threats don't work,' explained Pongwiffy knowledgeably to the fascinated audience.

She was right. They didn't. Neither did the Running Up And Down Hill, the Leaping Into The Air, the Twisting Around In Circles or the rasped orders to the Lads to Come To His Aid. None of the Familiars was prepared to risk it. This little

73

Hamster was quite something. He simply hung on and hung on with the sticking power of a limpet dipped in superglue – and finally, Dudley could take no more.

'All right! All right! May the whales whip yer whiskers out, what be it ye *want*?'

'Shay shorry,' said Hugo through a mouthful of stringy tail.

'Shan't. Meaaaaaaaaaah! All right, all right! I'm *sorry*, may ye be brained by a blunt cutlass!'

'Vat's my name?'

'Hugo, may ye be cuddled by an octopus!'

'Vat am I?'

'A Hamster! May ye be mobbed by stingrays!'

'Vat else?'

'Pongwiffy's Familiar, may ye be splatted by a rusty anchor!'

'Vat am I not?'

'A pet. A pet, a pet, a PET. Now, GET OFF MY TAIL!'

And Hugo let go. There was silence on the hill. Nobody could quite believe what they had just witnessed. Dead Eye Dudley, ex-pirate and leader of the Familiars, had been defeated by a Hamster. Dudley, aware of the shocked eyes, muttered something about having a bad back, and slunk off to lick his wounds. Sharkadder scuttled off after him, crying, 'I'll never speak to you again, Pongwiffy!'

Pongwiffy scooped Hugo up and held him triumphantly aloft. The Witches and their Familiars gave a great cheer and crowded in, full of admiration and congratulations, wanting to be the first to shake the new champion by the paw.

'He's small, I know,' babbled Pongwiffy. 'And sort of cute, I'm afraid. But he's got guts, and he does his best. That's what counts.'

Hugo sat on her shoulder, shaking hands and trying to look casual. But inside, he was glowing. He'd made the grade. He'd struck a blow for Hamsters everywhere. His future was mapped out, and he had a real career before him.

'Vat about anuzzer sandvich?' he said.

'Not a chance,' said Grandwitch Sourmuddle, crawling out from beneath an empty trestle table. 'I just finished the last one. And now I think it's time to cut my cake.'

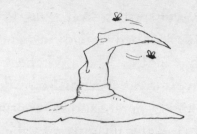

CHAPTER FIVE
Little Pieces of Paper

'These Meetings are always really boring,' complained Pongwiffy to Grandwitch Sourmuddle a few weeks later. 'Nothing exciting's happened since Hugo put Dudley in his place.'

Sourmuddle unclamped her toothless gums from a stale spiderspread sandwich and said, 'I'm sure this bread is left over from last month. I recognise the green speckly bits.'

'That's what I mean. Even the food's awful. All we ever do is eat old sandwiches and swap old news. Dull. Dull-dull-dull. Dull as ditchwater.'

'Ditchwater can be quite tasty at times. Depends what's swimming in it.' Sourmuddle dug out a green speckle of mould with a dirty fingernail and tasted it experimentally. 'Hmm. Definitely last month's, that.'

'We should do something different. For a change,' mused Pongwiffy. 'We ought to rack our brains and think of ideas. Write them down on little pieces of paper and put them in a hat. I'm sure something would come out of it.'

'I know what'd come out of it,' said Grandwitch Sourmuddle wisely.

'What?'

'Little pieces of paper. Tee hee hee.'

'Just a suggestion,' said Pongwiffy. 'But of course if you're happy to be Mistress of the most boring Coven in the whole world, that's up to you. Not everyone likes fun.'

'Me not like fun? Certainly I like fun. How dare you! I am a Fun-loving Person, and if you don't apologise I shall make your nose drop off. That'd be really funny.'

'Sorry,' said Pongwiffy quickly. She was fond of her nose.

'What for?' said Sourmuddle, who had already

forgotten. 'What were we talking about?'

'How boring our Meetings are,' explained Pongwiffy patiently. 'I was saying we should all put our heads together, and . . .'

'What, in a big pile, you mean? Then when the music stops we all rush in and grab one, and the one who doesn't . . .'

'No, no! I didn't mean that at all. It's just a figure of speech.'

'Oh. Pity. It sounded fun,' said Sourmuddle, disappointed. 'Though I'm not sure I know a head-removing spell. Not offhand. You'd need your head screwed on to think of a spell like that. Tee hee hee.'

Pongwiffy sighed. 'Look, forget about the heads, Sourmuddle. I only meant that we ought to come up with some suggestions for interesting things to do.'

'Oh, I *see*. To make the Meetings less boring, you mean. Wait a minute! We could think of some things to do which would be fun, and have a really good time!'

'Exactly!'

'What a good idea. I might be getting on a bit, but I do come up with these good ideas from time to time.'

'But it was my idea!' protested Pongwiffy.

'What was? Look, never mind about your idea now, Pongwiffy, let's concentrate on mine before I forget it. Everyone must come up with some suggestions. We'll put them in a hat and have a vote. Well? What are you waiting for? Organise it!'

So Pongwiffy organised it. A moment later, all the Witches on Crag Hill were surprised to find little pieces of paper and sharp red pencils suddenly appearing in their hands. They muttered uneasily, hoping it wasn't a spelling test.

Pongwiffy whisked Hugo away from an admiring group of Familiars, popped him on her shoulder and marched up to the bonfire.

'Quiet, everyone! I have something important to say. Grandwitch Sourmuddle and I have just been having a chat. These Meetings are really boring, and my idea is this . . .'

'*My* idea!' interrupted Sourmuddle, stamping her foot. 'Mine! Mine!'

'All right, then. Sourmuddle's-idea-which-she-pinched-from-me is this. Everyone has to come up with a suggestion and write it down and put it in my hat. Then we'll go through them, and decide on the best one.'

'What sort of suggestions?' asked several voices at once.

'That's up to you. Anything you think might be fun.'

'I know! I know!' screeched Witch Gaga. 'We can all hang upside-down from trees pretending to be bats. Or if it's a chestnut tree we can be nuts, or if it's a Christmas tree we can be crackers . . .'

'Yes, well, write it down, Gaga, write it down. Now, no more talking. You have exactly five minutes from NOW.'

There was a great deal of panicky shuffling. Witches went into huddles with their Familiars, crying things like, 'Stop looking! Macabre's trying to copy!' and 'My pencil's broken!' and 'How d'you spell bats?'

Five minutes later, Pongwiffy called time.

'Write your names on, then get in an orderly line. No pushing. Right, let's have your papers.'

In a disorderly mob and with a great deal of pushing, the Witches dropped their papers into Pongwiffy's upturned hat, then sat down again, looking expectant.

'Now then. Hugo will pass them to me one by

one, and I shall read them out. Clap if you like any of the ideas. First please, Hugo.'

Hugo dipped into the hat and passed the first paper to Pongwiffy. She smoothed it out and frowned.

'This is blank. Who handed in a blank piece of paper?'

'Me,' confessed Bonidle with a bored yawn.

'But everyone's supposed to have an idea! You've written nothing.'

'That's my idea. I like doing nothing. So there.' And Bonidle promptly went to sleep.

'Well, I don't think much of that. Any claps for that one?'

There were no claps for that one, so Pongwiffy moved on to the next. 'This one's Macabre's idea. It says *SING SCOTTISH BATTLE SONGS OR MUD WRESTLING*.'

'Aye. Ah thought o' two,' bragged Witch Macabre, and her Haggis gave her an admiring lick with his long purple tongue.

'But we don't know any Scottish battle songs, Macabre. And this mud wrestling business – I don't think any of us here fancy it much.'

'Aye, but Ah do.'

'Yes, Macabre, but you can't mud wrestle on your own, can you? Who'd win? The mud? Well, let's put it to the vote. Who wants to sing battle songs or mud wrestle with Macabre?' Nobody did, so she moved on.

'*EVERYONE BRINGS A BALLOON AND POPS IT*. That's the twins.' Agglebag and Bagaggle hugged each other and giggled.

'Well, it's not *bad*, I suppose,' said Pongwiffy doubtfully. 'Balloons are partyish sort of things . . .'

'No! No balloons! My granny got eaten by polar bears because of a balloon!' That was Sourmuddle.

'Dear, dear. Why was that?' enquired Pongwiffy politely.

'She collided with one of those hot air balloons she did, over the North Pole it was, punctured it with her broomstick she did, you could hear the explosion for miles around you could. Or was that my great-granny? Yes, come to think of it, it must have been Great-granny. Or was it someone else's granny? Fetch me another sandwich, Snoop. What was I saying?'

'Never mind,' said Pongwiffy heavily. 'No balloons. Next please, Hugo.'

'Mine next,' said Grandwitch Sourmuddle,

suddenly remembering what was happening.

'It's not your turn . . .'

'Who's Mistress of this Coven? Mine next.'

Muttering, Pongwiffy signalled to Hugo, who scrabbled around in the hat until he found Sourmuddle's paper.

'*HAVE A BIRTHDAY PARTY FOR SOURMUDDLE*,' read out Pongwiffy, and a vast sigh went up.

'Well, why not?' whined Sourmuddle.

'Because your birthday's still two months away. You've been told a hundred times.'

Sourmuddle went into a deep sulk, and Pongwiffy moved on.

The next idea was *BRING-AND-BUY SALE*. That was from Bendyshanks. Everyone wanted to know what a Bring-and-Buy Sale was. Bendyshanks said they all had to bring a load of Old Rubbish and buy it. The Witches wanted to know what sort of Old Rubbish. Bendyshanks said rags, old shoes, home-made cakes and jigsaws with half the pieces missing. Ratsnappy growled that it seemed daft, coming up with a load of Old Rubbish, then buying it straight back. Bendyshanks explained that the idea was to buy other people's Old Rubbish.

This provoked an outcry. Witches declared that

they wouldn't be seen dead in one of Pongwiffy's stinky old cardigans or a pair of Sludgegooey's shoes. And as for Gaga's home-made sponge with the cement filling – talk about instant death, one slice of that and it'd be a Bring-and-Die Sale. And so on and so on.

The Bring-and-Buy Sale was obviously doomed to failure, so Pongwiffy moved on to the next idea, which was *START A BROWNIE PACK*, suggested by Ratsnappy. This was roundly jeered as much too goody-goody.

Greymatter's *INTELYJENT SOCIETY FOR BRAINY WITCHES* didn't get a single clap because no one could spell intelligent.

Scrofula's *RAFFLE* proved equally unpopular when it was discovered that the prize would be a rare collection of Scrofula's old hairbrushes. Scrofula's dandruff was shocking. She had the most Christmassy shoulders in the world.

Gaga's idea of *HANGING FROM TREES* never got written down, because she was off somewhere hanging from one. That meant there was now only one remaining paper in the hat. It belonged to Sharkadder.

Now, it must be remembered that Sharkadder

was still upset about Hugo making her Dudley look foolish. Also, she had recently had another row with Pongwiffy. Something about missing hair rollers. In fact, she and Pongwiffy were currently worst enemies.

Sharkadder's paper said *MAKE-UP DEMONSTRATION*.

'Huh!' said Pongwiffy, reading it out with a sneer. 'Well, I think we all agree that's a terrible idea, so I'm afraid . . .'

'Hold it!' howled Sharkadder, outraged. 'You haven't given anyone a chance to clap! You saw that, everyone, she didn't even . . .'

'Oh, all right. Hands up anyone who in their right mind would volunteer to be made up by Sharkadder. Bearing in mind she uses wire wool for cleansing, which is why her own ugly mug looks like the surface of the moon. There, see? No one. Told you.'

Sharkadder flexed her long nails dangerously and said, 'Not so fast, ferret face. There's another suggestion on the other side.'

There was too. It said: *TIE PONGWIFFY TO A THORN BUSH AND THROW OLD TEA BAGS AT HER!*

'Suggest you do not read zis one out,' advised Hugo in a whisper. ' 'E might be popular.' Pongwiffy took his advice and accidentally on purpose dropped the paper in the fire. Sharkadder jumped up and down, snarling.

'Well, that's that,' said Pongwiffy, ignoring her. 'What a load of useless suggestions. I don't know why I bothered.'

'What about you, bug brain?' heckled Sharkadder. 'What's your idea?'

'I don't have to think of one. I organised it.'

'Boo!' howled the Witches, led by Sharkadder. 'Can't think of one!'

'Can,' snapped Pongwiffy, who couldn't. Her brains always seemed to be out whenever she called on them. Luckily, Hugo came to her rescue.

'I vish to speak.' There was immediate silence. For a new boy, Hugo commanded a great deal of respect. In fact, he was already well on his way to becoming leader of the Familiars, particularly since Dudley was still on the sick list.

'My Mistress 'ave an idea. A great idea.'

'I do? Oh – er – quite right,' agreed Pongwiffy. 'You tell them, Hugo. I'm shy.' And she listened with interest to what her idea was.

'*TALENT CONTEST*,' announced Hugo. 'Ze Great Talent Contest. Ze vinner vill vin a vunderful avard

86

vich I vill carve viz mine own paws. I shall call it ze 'Ugo Avard.'

'Eh? What's he talking about?' muttered the Witches, having trouble with all this talk of vinners and avards.

'He means the best act gets a prize,' translated Pongwiffy. 'I think.'

'Not only zat,' continued Hugo, warming to his subject and ignoring Pongwiffy, who was trying to shut him up. 'As well as prize, ze contest vill be judged by A Famous Person from ze vorld of show business. Ve vill send out invitations far and vide. Zis contest vill go down in 'istory!'

There was an awed silence.

'Idiot!' hissed Pongwiffy.

Suddenly, to Pongwiffy's astonishment, the silence erupted into a storm of applause. A talent contest! Of course. With an award, and a Famous Person judging it! What a good idea!

'It's a terrible idea, you stupid Hamster!' screamed Pongwiffy, the minute they were at home and in private. 'It's all very well for you. You go making all these rash promises, then I'm stuck with the

87

consequences. A Famous Person from the world of show business, my foot! Do *you* know anyone like that? I'm sure I don't. Except for a monkey I once knew who joined a circus, but I believe he's retired.'

'No problem,' said Hugo with a wink. He was sitting in a cracked teacup, making notes on the back of a postage stamp. 'Guess 'oo is at zis very moment 'olidaying at 'is castle retreat on ze uzzer side of Vitchvay Vood.'

'How should I know? Who?'

'Scott Sinister. Zat's 'oo. Zat'll be anuzzer contribution to ze 'Amsters Are Angry Cause, pliz.' Hugo had begun charging for Good Ideas.

'*What?*' Pongwiffy ripped the sleeve off her cardigan in her excitement. 'Scott Sinister? *The* Scott Sinister? Star of a thousand horror movies and *my dreamboat?*'

'Ze very same.'

'Oh, Hugo! Just imagine if Scott Sinister would come and judge our talent contest! I'd meet him in the flesh! I've always loved him, ever since I was a teenwitch. Oh, Scott, Scott!' Pongwiffy went into a trance, a soppy grin on her face.

'Zere you are, zen. No problem.'

'But how will we get him to agree? I mean, he's

88

on holiday, isn't he? He might not want to. Oh Scott, Scott, I've lost you!'

'Nonsense. Ve make him.'

'How? Gold? He's so rich he doesn't need it.'

'Nein. Sumpsink better. Blackmail.'

'*Blackmail?* Blackmail my Scott?'

'Ya.'

Pongwiffy thought about it. 'Hmm. Good idea,' she said.

'Zat'll be ten pence,' said Hugo.

CHAPTER SIX
Scott Sinister

Scott Sinister, Famous Star of stage and screen and Pongwiffy's dreamboat, was reclining in a purple silk hammock by the side of the large, coffin-shaped swimming pool which took up most of the castle grounds. He was wearing a gold dressing gown with S S embroidered across the front. Expensive (but silly) sunglasses shaded his Famous Red Eyes, gold chains dripped from his Famous White Throat, and gold fillings flashed as he picked at his Famous Fangs with a gold-plated toothpick. His Famous Feet nestled in fur-lined snakeskin slippers, and diamonds the size of ping-pong balls sparkled on his Famous Fingers.

To one side of him, there was a table piled high with rare delicacies – sweet pickles from the Lost Isle of Pan Yan, bogberries from the Misty Mountains, mole-flavoured yoghurt, and a great bucket of gorilla ice cream. On the other side a small, grim-faced Gnome in turban and swimming trunks held up a large crimson umbrella to protect the Famous Flesh from the sun. The Gnome also waved a fan around in a casual sort of way, giving the occasional slight clonk to the Famous Nose.

'Look, *do* you mind! Why can't you watch what you're doing?'

'OK, bud, OK,' said the Gnome, who was only temporary.

'I don't know what's happening to servants these days,' grumbled Scott Sinister to the starlet who was gently dabbing at his brow with a cloth dipped in perfumed water. 'Badness knows I pay them enough.' He took a sip from a glass containing something red with ice cubes, and gestured despairingly with a limp white hand. 'I mean, just look at those bodyguards. What a bunch! That's what comes of hiring the locals.'

The bunch consisted of several large Goblins in bobble hats, huge boots and grubby, tight-fitting dinner jackets. They stood around cracking their finger joints, fiddling with their bow ties and muttering in low voices. A bent, humpbacked figure in butler's uniform creaked about collecting dirty glasses. Two She-Goblins in blonde wigs sprawled by the side of the pool, lumpy bodies stuffed into pink bathing costumes, hoping to be in Scott Sinister's next film.

Just then, the biggest Goblin came up, obviously bursting with news. It is our old friend, Plugugly. Small world, isn't it?

''Scuse me, Mr Sinister,' said Plugugly. 'Dere's an 'amster at de main gate. Wants a word wiv yer.'

'A *Hamster*? Bad gracious, Goblin, who do you think I am? I'm on holiday, remember? I have better things to do than talk to rodents. Do you have any idea what it's like to be rich and famous and extremely bad-looking? Well, I'll tell you. It's exhausting. That toothpaste commercial was the last straw. I am tired, Goblin. Tired, weary, strained, tense, jaded, drained and totally pooped. I hired you to protect me from my adoring public, so go and do it! Hurry up, step on it!'

'Step on it? Right, sir.'

Plugugly bowed as deeply as his belly would let him. All the buttons burst from his dinner jacket and rolled into the swimming pool. Plop, plop, plop, plop, plop. Plugugly waddled away, looking vexed.

'Now, perhaps I can relax a little. Lulu, my darling, pass me one of those marzipan frogs. No, on second thoughts, I think I'll have a nap. I've already been up two hours – how much more can my body take? But first, pass me that mirror. I haven't looked at myself for ages. I've told you before, Gnome, keep that fan *moving*!'

Before Lulu could pass the mirror, Plugugly was back again, jacket flapping messily and a grubby-looking envelope in his hand.

''Ate ter bovver yer again, Mr Sinister, sir,' he said. 'I tried ter step on it, but it threatened to bite me. It give me a letter fer yer. It's waitin' fer a – what were it again? Oh yer – reply.'

'Stubborn little beast, isn't it? Oh, give it here, then. Fan mail, I suppose.'

'In that case, fan yourself with it,' said the Gnome, throwing down both umbrella and fan and walking out in a huff.

'That's right! Go and sit by a pond somewhere

– it's all you're fit for anyway! That's the last time I hire a Gnome. I'd sooner be gnomeless. Ha ha! Hear what I just said, Lulu?'

Pleased with himself, Scott Sinister slit the envelope with a filed fingernail and took out a filthy piece of paper. His good mood didn't last long. In Pongwiffy's best writing, the note said:

Dear Scott Sinister,

You don't no me, but I am your biggest fan. I have sin all yore films. I liked you best as the daddy in The Rampaging Mummy. Now, heer is my rekwest. Plese will you come and judge our talent contest in witchway hall next friday. I no you will agree to do this becos you are such a kind and wunderfull person. Also I don't think you would like to wake up tomoro morning and find yore wunderfull swiming pool full of dead rats.

Yore bigest fan
Pongwiffy (Witch)
P.S. can I have yore autograrf?

'Blackmail! That's what it is! These Witches think they can get away with anything!' cried Scott Sinister, throwing down the letter in a fit of pique.

'Oh, I dunno,' said Plugugly, picking it up and peering at it. 'It's dirty, yer, but not exackly black. More grey. Yer, grey mail's what I'd call it.'

He was quite surprised when he found himself at the bottom of the swimming pool. But at least he found two of his buttons.

'I shall frame it,' said Pongwiffy happily, re-reading the letter from Scott Sinister for the umpteenth time that evening. 'I shall hang it on the wall over my bed and charge people to come and look. Just think, Hugo. He touched this paper with his own hands. Oh, Scott, Scott!'

There was a knock on the door. Agglebag and Bagaggle had come to enquire if it really was true that Scott Sinister had agreed to judge the contest, and please could they see the letter.

'Yes, it's true, and no, you can't,' said Pongwiffy. 'Not unless you give me ten pence each. Make that twenty and I'll let you touch it.'

The twins humbly paid up and stood gazing at the letter in awe. It was written on scarlet notepaper with gold edging, and said, in big black letters,

Dear Blackmailer,
I suppose so.
Yours sincerely,
Scott Sinister

'It doesn't say much, but I think he likes me,' said Pongwiffy shyly. 'See where he says he's mine sincerely?'

The next week was a waking nightmare. Pongwiffy's head was buzzing with all the things she had to think about and organise, and her hand nearly fell off with writing so many lists, all of which she lost.

'Hugo! Where's the list of acts? Here it is . . . no, that's a shopping list. Oh bother, I'm going to have to make a list of these lists . . .'

Calmly, Hugo handed her the list of acts. It included the name of every Witch in the Coven apart from Pongwiffy, who was the organiser, and wasn't taking part. It went like this:

Agglebag and Bagaggle: A Moosikal Dewet
Bendyshanks: Tap Dansing on Roler Skates
Bonidle: Koodunt Kare Less

Gaga: Mad Histirikal Laffing
Greymatter: A Pome
Macabre: Sumthing Scottish
Ratsnappy: Funny Jokes
Scrofula: Ventrillokwissum
Sludgegooey: Impreshuns
Sharkadder: Mak-up Demonstrayshun
Sourmuddle: A Sekret Song

Pongwiffy examined it doubtfully. 'You know, I'm not at all sure about Gaga's act. Mad, hysterical laughing. She does that all the time anyway.'

'Ah, but not in costume,' pointed out Hugo.

'Hmm. Where's my list? The one with all my duties on?'

Hugo handed it to her. It said:

Pongwiffy: Stayg Manijer, Prodewser,
Moosikal Direktor, Props, Programs,
Liting, Box ofiss, Compair,
Publissity, Everything Else

'It's no good,' said Pongwiffy, looking at it. 'I simply can't cope.' And she couldn't. The responsibility of it all and the thought that she was to meet Scott Sinister in the flesh proved too much. She wasted a lot of time making a frame for The Letter, then made herself sick with excitement and had to go to bed.

Hugo took over. He held a meeting with the other Familiars, but they didn't waste time making lists. Instead, they got right out and did the job – some of them providing the brains and others the brawn. They organised the benches in Witchway Hall, ordered the Brooms to sweep the stage, got the lights working, stopped the curtains sticking, had the piano tuned, got the programmes and *NO GOBLINS* posters printed, sold the tickets, ordered the ice cream and booked the band.

All these things could have been done by Magic if the Witches had been prepared to put their minds to it – but they were far too busy rehearsing their acts to worry about such dull, practical matters. The smell of greasepaint was in the air, and they all had visions of receiving the Hugo Award from Scott Sinister's own hands (to thunderous applause, naturally).

Some of them took to wearing dark glasses and claiming that they wanted to be alone, in between trying to get themselves photographed for *The Daily*

Miracle. Even Bonidle entered into the spirit of things, changing her act from *KOODUNT KARE LESS* to *UNICYCLING*. No one had seen the unicycle, but she could be seen from time to time limping home from some secret place swathed in bandages.

All the Witches kept the details of their acts a close secret. You might have heard a few mysterious noises coming from various caves and cottages as you strolled through the Wood, but that was all. Nobody really knew what anyone else was doing, and the atmosphere was charged with tension and excitement. Pongwiffy, meanwhile, lay in bed cuddling The Letter and counting the minutes.

'I make it only another two thousand eight hundred and eighty-two to go, Hugo,' she said dreamily some days later. Hugo was putting the final touches to the Hugo Award, which was a small statue of a Hamster holding a torch aloft. It was rather good except that the gold paint tended to rub off (being cheap cut-price stuff from Macabre's uncle, who was in the trade).

'Two tousant eight 'undred and eighty-two vat?'

'Minutes to go. Till I meet Scott Sinister.'

'Oh ya? Sumpsink up wiz your maths, I sink.'

'Why? How many do you make it?'

'Sixty.'

'WHAT? You're wrong. You must be!'

'Is true. Is now fifty-nine. You 'ave been fast asleep for two days. Better get out of bed. Tonight's ze night!'

He was right. It was.

Witchway Hall was packed. News of the Great Talent Contest had spread far and wide, and the tickets had been snapped up like hot cakes. A party of Skeletons had arrived in a hired hearse, talking loudly in snooty voices about the poor quality of entertainment on offer these days. Nevertheless they sat in the most expensive seats.

There was a bit of fuss when ticket holders found their seats already occupied by Ghouls who had sneaked in through the walls when nobody was looking, but Dead Eye Dudley was the bouncer, and managed to sort it out to everyone's dissatisfaction.

A row of Banshees shrieked and howled to each other in the back row, passing sweets and ignoring the glares from the rest of the audience. Fiends, Demons, Trolls, Bogeymen, Werewolves and even a couple of Wizards (in disguise, of course – it wouldn't do to be seen at a Witch Do) packed the hall.

The band began to unpack their instruments. They were called the Witchway Rhythm Boys, and consisted of a small Dragon named Arthur who played the piano, a Leprechaun named O'Brian on penny whistle and Filth the Fiend on drums. They were a long time tuning up, and the audience was getting restless.

'Why don't you play a proper tune?' screamed one of the Banshees in the back row.

'We just did,' said Arthur.

Meanwhile, Pongwiffy was biting her fingernails outside the hall. The Guest of Honour and Judge of the Contest still hadn't arrived. Suppose he didn't turn up? Suppose he was ill, or his coach had broken down, or he'd lost the address, or forgotten the day, or ... Suddenly, her heart leapt at the welcome sound of drumming hooves and a cracking whip.

Into the glade galloped a team of plumed, snorting, sweating coal black horses, towing behind them a long, low, gaudily painted coach. A huge star decorated the door, and the number plate read SSI. Scott Sinister had arrived!

Pongwiffy gave a muffled little scream of excitement as the coachman shuffled round to the door and wrenched it open with a flourish. Out stepped the great man, wearing an imposing gold and scarlet cloak, black fingerless gloves (to show off the rings) and a pair of rather silly sunglasses. Moonlight glinted off his sharp white teeth and his swinging medallions.

Pongwiffy stepped forward and dropped a deep, wobbling curtsy. Her heel caught in her hem, and there was a nasty tearing sound. It didn't matter – holes were a feature of the dress.

'Mr Sinister – may I call you Scott? I feel I know you so well. Scott, this is indeed an honour. I am Witch Pongwiffy, your humble fan.'

'Hmm. So you're the hag who threatened to put rats in my pool,' said Scott Sinister coldly.

'I am,' confessed Pongwiffy. 'But I wouldn't have done it, you know. Not really. I think you're wonderful. It seemed the only way to get you here. So let's forget all about it. I don't want anything to spoil this wonderful moment.'

Just then, something did spoil the wonderful moment. Lulu the starlet stepped from the coach, dripping with jewels and wearing a white evening gown. She was followed by Plugugly, with whom, as we know, Pongwiffy has had dealings in the past.

'My entourage,' said Scott Sinister haughtily. 'I never go anywhere without them.'

'Oh? Well, that's a pity, Scott, because, you see, we don't allow Goblins in Witch Territory.'

Pongwiffy gave her Wand a casual little wave, and Plugugly vanished with a howl of protest. All that was left of him was a sad little pile of buttons and an egg-stained bow tie, which fluttered to the ground like an ailing butterfly.

'Darling, who is this smelly old woman?' enquired Lulu, fluttering her eyelashes.

'Pongwiffy. Cheerio,' said Pongwiffy rudely, waving her Wand again. Lulu disappeared with a startled little scream. Her jewels remained behind, however, and Pongwiffy picked them up and popped them into her pocket – just for safe keeping, naturally.

'We have a rule about stuck-up hussies in nighties too,' she explained to Scott Sinister, who had gone *really* pale. 'Isn't this nice? I've got you all to myself.' And linking her arm with his, she propelled him firmly towards the hall.

There was a great deal of oohing and ahhing,

nudging and whispering and scattered applause as Pongwiffy, bursting with pride, escorted the famous star up the gangway to the seat of honour slap in the middle of the front row. You could tell it was the seat of honour because it was the only one with a cushion.

Scott Sinister swallowed hard as he peered around at the assembled audience. He was used to horrifying sights in his profession, but never had he seen such a grisly mob as this. To give him his due, though, he kept his head, and managed a limp wave and a bow or two before Pongwiffy shoved him impatiently into the special chair. There he sat, chewing his nails nervously, wondering what he'd let himself in for.

Pongwiffy, in her role as compère, scuttled up to the stage and began what was intended to be a very long opening speech.

'Ladies and Gentlemen, Fiends, Demons and Bogeymen, lend me your ears,' she said importantly. 'Thank you for coming. We're very honoured to have here tonight Mr Scott Sinister, who will judge the first ever Witch Talent Contest to be held in the history of the universe.'

'Hooray!' enthused the audience, throwing crisp

bags around.

'It was me who thought of getting him, you know,' went on Pongwiffy. 'In fact, this whole talent contest which you are about to enjoy was my idea, and I'd just like to say a few words about how I . . .'

'Boo!'

'Siddown!'

'Gerronwivit!'

'Oh, all right,' said Pongwiffy sulkily. 'Have it your own way. Is the first act ready back there, Hugo?'

A muffled squeak came from behind the closed curtains.

'Right. Well, the first act is Agglebag and Bagaggle, who will play a musical duet. Take it away, boys!'

The Witchway Rhythm Boys took it away and played a few bars of something rather horrible. Pongwiffy scurried to her chair which was set in the wings, the house lights dimmed, and the Great Talent Contest finally began.

CHAPTER SEVEN
The Contest

The curtains creaked apart to reveal the twins standing side by side centre stage, violins beneath their chins. They were wearing identical spotted scarves tied round their brows, identical swirly skirts and identical expressions of stage fright. Nothing happened for ages. The audience sniggered unkindly.

'Get on with it!' hissed Pongwiffy from the wings. 'Do something, idiots.' Each twin gave an identical nervous cough and an identical nervous shuffle. They nudged each other several times, and finally, much to everyone's relief, Agglebag spoke.

'This is a song about Witchway Wood. Sh-she wrote the words.'

'And sh-she wrote the music,' added Bagaggle.

'I sing the first verse, and she plays v-violin.'

'And I sing the second, and *she* plays v-violin.' They hesitated a moment, and looked at each other.

'But first, we both play violin,' they chorused together, and did. It was awful, but then it always was. After scraping away together a bit, Agglebag lowered her violin and sang her verse in a throaty voice.

'*Witchway Wood is really good,*' sang Agglebag.

'*Doo witchy doo witchy doo,*' sang Bagaggle, scraping away.

'*Much much better than Christmas pud,*' sang Agglebag.

'*Doo witchy doo witchy doo,*' obliged Bagaggle, then they both leapt about a bit, swirling their skirts and stamping. Then Bagaggle sang her verse.

'*Witchway Wood is where I'll be,*' she trilled.

'*Doo witchy doo witchy doo,*' carolled Agglebag, scraping. Then there was a pause.

'I've forgotten the next bit, Ag,' confessed Bagaggle, and burst into tears.

'Hooray!' thundered the audience in relief, and clapped their approval. The twins, assuming the applause meant they had gone down well, curtsied shyly and skipped off with their arms around each other while Hugo closed the curtains.

'Didn't we do well?' they asked Pongwiffy.

'Hmmm,' said Pongwiffy doubtfully, and went to announce the next act. This was Bendyshanks' roller-skating tap dance.

The Witchway Rhythm Boys struck up, the curtains wobbled open, Filth played an impressive drum roll, and Bendyshanks zoomed on stage. There was a lot of smoke coming from her heels. In fact, they appeared to be seriously on fire. She was wearing a crash helmet, and her bandy old legs sported red, white and blue shin pads.

The audience only had a fleeting glimpse of the outfit, however, for not only did Bendyshanks zoom on stage, she zoomed straight off it again, falling like a stone straight into the orchestra pit where the Witchway Rhythm Boys were playing merry Roller Skating Tap Dance Music.

Her head went straight through Filth's drum and she had to be carried out with her thin legs in their jolly shin pads kicking feebly in the air. At least everyone got a good look at the Special Custom-Built Super-Charged Roller Skates With Attached Rocket Launcher just before they exploded. When they did, the audience went wild. Scott Sinister yawned and looked at his watch.

'Bonidle will now perform on her Unicycle,' announced Pongwiffy over the uproar. Everyone sat up, interested, for nobody had yet seen the famous Unicycle.

When it finally wobbled from the wings, with Bonidle perched precariously on top, it was indeed an impressive sight, consisting mainly of an old cartwheel with a makeshift seat arrangement tied somehow on the top with string. However, the best bit was undoubtedly the handlebars.

Everyone agreed about that. Bonidle had gone to town on these. They were covered with fur and dripping with lights, bells, good luck charms and things that bobbed up and down on elastic. They also appeared to be playing 'Jingle Bells' (a rather clever inbuilt stereo system).

The only thing they didn't have was brakes. Bonidle hadn't bothered to fit any, having lost interest towards the end. This was rather a pity, because there's little point in wasting long, painful hours mastering the Art of Balance unless you also master the Art of Stopping.

Bonidle merely wobbled relentlessly onwards, ending up (you've guessed it) in the orchestra pit, together with her Unicycle which promptly came adrift. Another drum was ruined, O'Brian's penny whistle got bent, Bonidle was carried off for first aid treatment muttering, 'Who cares anyway?' and the audience brought the roof down. Scott Sinister closed his eyes.

'The next act is Mad Hysterical Laughing from Gaga,' announced Pongwiffy, when order was once again restored. 'I'm afraid.' The audience looked puzzled. It sounded an odd sort of act.

It was. The curtains parted to reveal a huge cardboard box painted with wild, crazy colours, sitting in the middle of the stage. Out of this burst Gaga, decked in a very strange outfit of paper flowers, ribbons, and huge safety pins. She had a clothes peg on her nose and a basket of bananas on her head. What looked like large stuffed parrots swung from her ears, and her feet were jammed into bright yellow wellington boots. The effect was most unusual.

The Mad Hysterical Laughing wasn't, though. It was exactly the same as always, just as Pongwiffy had predicted. After several minutes of watching Gaga prance about cackling and waving her yellow boots, Pongwiffy gave a signal, and the colourfully

garbed performer, still doubled up with mirth, was forcibly removed by two of the larger Familiars. The audience, after hesitating, decided to give her a clap for originality, so that was all right. Scott Sinister, however, was fast asleep.

'A poem by Greymatter, Our Very Own Thinking Witch,' bawled Pongwiffy. 'Thank goodness,' she added to Hugo. 'A bit of class won't hurt after that lot.'

The Brains of the Coven walked on stage, poem in hand. Her Witch hat had been replaced by a mortar board. Grimly, she adjusted her glasses and spoke in a stern, headmistressy way, which had everyone hiding their sweets and paying attention.

'Right, sit up straight. This poem is entitled *Hard Words*. I suspect it's way beyond you, but I can't help being clever. So here goes . . .

'HARD WORDS
Adenoids, apothecary,
Symbolise, constabulary,
Oxidise, preliminary,
Psychic buffalo,
Peek-a-boo and barbecue,
Here's a French one, rendezvous.

These are but a sample
Of the hardest words I know.'

Greymatter walked off to a storm of applause. Nobody had understood a word, but they all thought that if they clapped hard enough, everyone else would think they had.

Next came Macabre who, you may remember, was planning Something Scottish. The curtains opened, and the audience gasped. Macabre, whose uncle was in the paint trade, had painted a huge backcloth depicting a Scottish Glen. There was a lot of swirling purple (heather), swirling grey (sky), and yellow blobs (sheep – her uncle couldn't get hold of white).

In the midst of this Highland Scene was Macabre in full Scottish rig-out, mounted on her Haggis, who had a ton of heather plaited into his orange fringe and was draped with much tartan cloth. His head sported a peculiar sort of hat thing which was apparently Traditional Haggis Ceremonial Headgear. He snorted and shook his fringe proudly, pawing the boards while Macabre, wearing so much clashing tartan that the audience saw squares for a week, blew into her bagpipes, intending to treat the assembled company to a rousing chorus of 'Scotland the Brave'.

Unfortunately, somebody had Sabotaged The Bagpipes. We won't say who, because it really was a terribly mean thing to do. But the fact remains that somebody (armed with a knitting needle or something similar) had attacked those bagpipes in the still of the night and punctured them very thoroughly. In fact, they had more holes than a fishing net.

The minute Macabre blew, they gave a sad little puffing wheeze and then gave in and died. Macabre, taken aback, shook them, attempted the kiss of life, then gave vent to such a disgraceful stream of Scottish Bad Words that the audience were enthralled. The Haggis, also outraged, reared up, steam hissing from its nostrils, and let out a bitter moo.

'Ah'll find oot!' raged Macabre, waving her Ceremonial Sword aloft. 'Ah'll find oot who murdered ma pipes if it's the last thing Ah do!'

And she hurled the useless bagpipes into the audience. They landed on Scott Sinister, but he didn't wake up. She dug in her heels and galloped off stage, howling doom and destruction.

What an act! What could follow that but the interval? The audience fell upon the ice cream with cries of delight and contentedly stuffed themselves, talking about how much they were enjoying it. These Witches could certainly put on a show. Even the Skeletons said it wasn't bad, they supposed.

Ten minutes later Pongwiffy called time and the audience waded back to their seats through a sea of bogberry ripple and buzzed excitedly as the second half began.

The first act after the interval was Ratsnappy. She was dressed as a clown in a shiny suit with bobbles attached. She had done her best, but the wide red smile painted on her face did little to disguise her usual expression of chronic bad temper.

'Who held a party in the haunted house?' she growled.

'We don't know! Tell us!' screamed the crowd.

'Who d'you think?' snarled Ratsnappy. 'The ghostess. Here's another. What d'you say to a two-headed monster? Hallo hallo.'

'Hear that? Hallo hallo! Get it? Oh ha ha ha!' roared the audience.

Ratsnappy, who only knew two jokes, signalled to the band to begin playing so that she could do

115

the Funny Dance she had worked out. Sadly, she had only finished making her long clown shoes that morning, and hadn't actually practised dancing in them. She only managed to do three hops and a twirl before falling flat on her face. She was carried off unconscious. The audience, convinced this was all part of the act, gave her a standing ovation.

Scrofula came next, sitting on a stool with her hand in a holey sock.

'Gottle of geer, gottle of geer,' ground out Scrofula through gritted teeth, and waggled her fingers a bit, to make the sock look like it was talking.

'Hello, everygoggy, gy game ish Fred.' (Get that?)

'Saw your lips move,' shouted one of the Banshees.

'Gno you giggen.' (No you didn't.)

'Yes we did.' (Yes we did.)

'Gno you giggen!' (No you didn't!)

'Yes we did!' (Yes we did!)

'Giggen! Giggen!' (Didn't! Didn't!)

'Gig! Gig!' (Did! Did!)

It was all great fun, and everyone was disappointed when Scrofula wiggled her fingers just that bit too hard and the sock fell apart. No more sock, no more act – but everyone agreed that it had been wonderful while it lasted, and Scrofula took bow after triumphant bow.

Time now for Sludgegooey's Impressions. These proved enormously popular, because the impressions were all of her fellow Witches. She did Sharkadder making-up, Pongwiffy scenting a rubbish tip, Bonidle getting up in the morning, and Gaga trying to add up a milk bill. She never got any further than that, because Sharkadder, Pongwiffy, Bonidle and Gaga marched on stage looking very put out, and bundled her off, much to the displeasure of the audience, who had loved it so far and wanted to see the rest. At this point, Scott Sinister woke up, checked his programme, and was relieved to see that there were only two acts to go.

Sharkadder's Make-up Demonstration was next. The curtains parted, revealing a large table set out with mirrors, dozens of little pots, lipsticks, brushes, jars, combs and hair grips. Beneath the table was a huge bucket full of hot mud. Sharkadder, wearing orange ribbons, a shocking pink evening gown and so much rouge that it hurt to look at her, waltzed to the front of the stage and asked for a volunteer.

The audience with one accord shrank into their

seats. Some went so far as to get down on hands and knees pretending they'd dropped their programmes, so anxious were they not to volunteer. In the wings, Pongwiffy sniggered. Sharkadder heard.

'I thought of demonstrating on Pongwiffy,' Sharkadder told the audience maliciously. 'But there really doesn't seem much point. It would be like putting a fresh coat of paint on a very old, cracked wall. So perhaps . . .' she added sweetly. 'Perhaps our distinguished guest would oblige. Up you come, Mr Sinister!'

Scott Sinister was too much of a showman to refuse. With a tolerant smile he stood, graciously acknowledged the cheers of the audience and made his way to the stage, sinking elegantly into the chair Sharkadder had set ready. He glanced into the wings and suddenly began to get a bit worried by the sight of Pongwiffy shaking her head and mouthing, 'No! No!' with a desperate expression on her face.

'Look, I really don't think . . .' said Scott Sinister, attempting to rise.

'Too late, Mr Sinister, you're mine now,' trilled Sharkadder gaily, giving him a rough push and draping a towel around his neck. 'Now, everybody, pay close attention, for I am about to demonstrate deep cleansing. For this, I use hot mud.' And she scooped a large handful from the bucket and slapped it on Scott Sinister's face. It wasn't a pleasant experience. Firstly, it was uncomfortably hot, and secondly, a great deal of it went into his mouth.

'Groooougghch!' spluttered Scott Sinister. 'Get . . . it . . . off!'

'Patience, Mr Sinister,' sang Sharkadder brightly. 'We must wait a moment and let the cooling mudpack do its work, drawing out all the little impurities and hidden gunk that you never knew you had. Right, that should be long enough. Now, everybody, you will observe that I take this old rag and wipe it off, leaving a beautifully radiant skin, glowing with cleanliness.'

And Sharkadder attempted to wipe off the mud. And this is the point at which she came unstuck.

And the reason she became unstuck is that the mud didn't. It didn't seem to want to shift at all. It remained firmly welded in a great glob to the famous Sinister face.

And the reason that it wouldn't wipe off is because, unbeknown to Sharkadder, Pongwiffy had dropped in just a few drops of Stickee Kwickee

Super-Duper Glue, the advertising slogan of which is 'Falling apart? Gum and stick with us'.

It was lethal stuff, instant and long-lasting, and it was very wrong of Pongwiffy to have put it in Sharkadder's cleansing mud.

Of course, she had had a great deal of provocation since the affair of the missing hair rollers, which she genuinely hadn't taken. In fact, the hedgehogs had roused themselves enough one night to crawl off home by themselves. Sharkadder had accused Pongwiffy of stealing them, and written PONGWIFFY IS A THEEF in lipstick on tree trunks all over the Wood, which was of course untrue.

So, although Pongwiffy has behaved very badly and had no right to spoil Sharkadder's chance of winning the Hugo award by playing such an underhand trick, perhaps we'll let her off. Particularly as the trick has misfired so badly and her beloved Scott is now thickly coated in a mud pack which has gone from globby to rock hard in seconds.

'Mmmmph!' wailed Scott Sinister, from somewhere underneath.

'Keep calm, Mr Sinister. Can you hear me in there? I'm rubbing as hard as I can . . . It's funny,

I can't get it off my hand either . . .' cried poor Sharkadder, who still hadn't twigged what had happened.

'Oh no! Oh no!' moaned Pongwiffy in the wings, rocking to and fro in horror as her idol flung himself from the chair and began to flail blindly about the stage, muttering, 'grooo' and 'blurk' and other muffled things like that. Pongwiffy had made the bad mistake, you see, of assuming that as usual Sharkadder would fail to get a volunteer and end up demonstrating on herself.

In the process of rocking, Pongwiffy's hat fell off, which was a pity because that was where she had hidden the tube of Stickee Kwickee after carrying out the evil deed.

'Aha!' screamed Sharkadder, seeing it fall. 'Now I get it!' And that's when it all got out of control. Sharkadder scooped up a handful of mud and hurled it at Pongwiffy. It caught her slap in the left eye. Pongwiffy screeched and threw herself on Sharkadder. They rolled around the stage, tipping over the bucket of mud. It glopped all over the place. Huge cheers came from the audience.

Scott Sinister, still staggering around, slipped in the hot mud flowing from the bucket and fell (you've got it) into the orchestra pit, putting his foot through Filth's one remaining drum and splattering the audience with glue-spiked mud.

Of course, the audience retaliated with ice cream, programmes, benches and anything they could lay their hands on. Macabre came galloping back down the aisle on her Haggis, thinking it was straightforward mud wrestling. Witches and Familiars poured from backstage and waded in with a will. Within seconds the hall was in total uproar.

To crown it all, poor old Grandwitch Sourmuddle was standing on Sharkadder's table wearing a yellow party frock and singing 'Happy Birthday', which of course was the surprise song which she hadn't had the chance to sing. Nobody noticed, which was rather sad. After all, she was very old and Mistress of the Coven.

And that was the end of the Great Talent Contest, if not the end of the evening. The end of the evening was a disgrace to all concerned, and we won't bother to describe it.

Several days later, Pongwiffy, still very sore from the special solvent she had used to remove the congealed mud from her left eye, legs and, I'm afraid, bottom, lay in her sickbed and stared sadly at the second letter from Scott Sinister. What it said doesn't bear repeating.

'I don't think I'll have it framed,' she said sadly.

'I vouldn't,' agreed Hugo.

'It's such a pity it ended like that. Nobody got your Hugo Award. And he'll never speak to me again. When they chipped it off, one of his fangs came out, you know. Oh Scott, Scott! It's all my fault.' And Pongwiffy burst into tears.

'Cheer up, Mistress,' said Hugo. ' 'Ere. For you.' He handed Pongwiffy a little box. In it was the Hugo Award.

'Oh, thanks, Hugo,' said Pongwiffy, pleased. 'You're a good little chap. By the way, did you take that solvent round to Sharky?'

'Ya, but she von't use it. She say she vait and get her own. Still she not speak to you.'

'Talk about bearing a grudge. All this time later, and she still hasn't forgiven me. You know what she is?'

'Vat?'

'Stuck-up,' said Pongwiffy. Which was true.

CHAPTER EIGHT
Preparations

Sourmuddle's two hundredth birthday was only a week away. Sourmuddle seemed to have forgotten all about it, which was a funny thing considering that was all she ever seemed to talk about. It was probably because she had been wrong about the date so many times she had given up hope of it ever arriving.

The Witches were determined that her party was going to be a Really Good Do. It was an important occasion, not just because reaching two hundred deserves celebration, but because

Sourmuddle had often hinted that she intended to retire at two hundred, which meant she would have to name her successor as Mistress of the Coven.

All the Witches fancied the job because of the perks. These included: unlimited credit at Malpractiss Magic Ltd, the shop where the Witches bought all their equipment; a new Broom with a year's free service, including a complete bristle change and respray; a rather desirable two-up-two-down cottage in a better part of the Wood; three weeks' paid holiday; trial offers of every new magic powder that came on the market and an annual invitation to the Monster Ball. Best of all, you could boss everyone around, which was the real reason why everyone wanted the job.

Grandwitch Sourmuddle had noticed that everyone was avoiding her. Wherever she went, Witches were whispering and going into huddles. All this talking behind her back worried her so much that she became convinced that everyone was plotting a mutiny against her. She got so nervous about it, she confiscated all Wands, claiming that she wanted to check them for Wand rot. At least the enemy was now deprived of their main weapons. She then barricaded herself into her cottage and set about weaving complicated spells designed to protect herself when the revolution came. This was good, because it meant the Witches were free to get to work planning her surprise party.

There was a lot of quarrelling as usual, because all of them wanted to be seen doing the most important job, which would be another point in their favour when Sourmuddle decided who should step into her boots as Grandwitch.

The thing that caused the most argument was The Cake. After all, apart from cards and presents it's The Cake that makes a birthday seem like a birthday. Each Witch was convinced that she was the best cook for miles around, and wanted the glory of making Sourmuddle's cake. The row was really beginning to get out of hand when Sharkadder put an end to it by suggesting that the fairest thing would be to have a collection and buy one, and that she would have a word with Pierre de Gingerbeard, the famous chef, who just happened to be her cousin.

This commanded a respectful silence. Everybody had heard of the great Pierre de Gingerbeard, author of *Buttered Snails and Other Tales*. Why, even the Wizards begged him to cook for their banquets! Fancy Sharkadder being related to him! Even Pongwiffy was impressed, and glad that she and Sharkadder were best friends. Yes, they were friends again. Pongwiffy had unravelled one of her old cardigans and knitted Dudley a blanket for his cat basket. He refused to use it, but the thought was there, and Sharkadder's heart had melted in no time.

'So it's decided, then,' said Sharkadder. 'I'll go and order it tomorrow. You can come with me, Pong.'

'Oh thanks, Sharky,' beamed Pongwiffy. 'I'd like that.' After all, helping order The Cake was an important job.

So the final list was drawn up of who should be responsible for what. It went like this:

Agglebag and Bagaggle – Music
Bendyshanks and Bonidle – Decorashuns
Gaga – Crackers, Crazy Hats
Greymatter and Macabre – Games
Ratsnappy, Scrofula and Sludgegooey – Food
Sharkadder and Pongwiffy – The Kake

And everyone was happy. Until the collection hat came round, that is. But then, you'd expect that, wouldn't you?

'Ooo? Ooo deed you say you are?' The barrel-shaped Dwarf with the tall white hat and the famous curling ginger beard peered at them with suspicious little currenty eyes. He sat at a small table in the middle of the great Gingerbeard Kitchens, stumpy little fingers nimbly moulding green marzipan frogs which he carefully placed in fancy boxes. They were so lifelike, those frogs, you could almost imagine them leaping out of their little paper nests and straight into your mouth.

'Sharkadder, Cousin Pierre,' explained Sharkadder for the third time, 'I used to sit on your knee. At family get-togethers.'

'Seet on my knee? You? Ees a joke, oui?'

'Well, of course I was little at the time. Look, surely you remember . . .'

Pongwiffy shuffled and whistled a little tune. The truth is, she was embarrassed. Early that morning, she and Sharkadder had set off for the Gingerbeard Kitchens. That's the name given to those huge caverns lying deep in the heart of the Misty Mountains where Pierre de Gingerbeard, famous chef, rules OK.

It was a long climb. As they had puffed up the steep slope, Pongwiffy had gaily prattled on

128

to Sharkadder about how wonderful it was that Sharkadder was related to the famous chef, and why hadn't she mentioned it before, it wasn't like her to be so modest, etc., etc.

Sharkadder had got quieter and quieter, and finally confessed that actually, they weren't *that* closely related. Pongwiffy remarked that cousins were quite close. Sharkadder said it depended on how many times removed. Pongwiffy asked how many times removed. Sharkadder said she'd forgotten, but a few times. Pongwiffy pressed for the exact number of times. Sharkadder said twenty-four, actually, but she always sent him a Christmas card, and she was sure he'd remember her. Pongwiffy announced that she wanted to go home, at which point Sharkadder sulked. Pongwiffy sulked harder. Sharkadder went all sad and finally burst into tears, so in the end Pongwiffy had agreed to accompany her, more, it must be confessed, because of the wonderful smell of baking wafting down the mountain than any thoughts of loyalty or friendship.

So there they were in the famous Gingerbeard Kitchens. Everywhere was hustle and bustle, with sweating Dwarfs stoking the great ovens into which went huge trays of pies, tarts, loaves

129

and cakes. More Dwarfs scurried to and fro with trays of eclairs, doughnuts and cherry slices balanced on their heads. Massive vats of chocolate bubbled and boiled, stirred and fussed over by the chocolate chefs; pastry chefs were pummelling dough with huge red hands; buckets of thick, rich cream were lined up half submerged in troughs of cool water; sacks of flour and sugar were being heaved about and shelves groaned under the weight of big pots of jam. The air was redolent with the most wonderful warm, sugary baking smell. Pongwiffy sniffed and drooled, desperately hoping that Pierre de Gingerbeard might offer them a few samples. But he hadn't so far.

'You see, my mother's auntie was your father's nephew's niece's fifth cousin twice removed on my granny's side . . .' Sharkadder was explaining again, wriggling uncomfortably as the sceptical little currant eyes bore into her.

'We are rrrelated? You are a cuzain of mine?'

'Yes. Isn't it fun?' said Sharkadder with a merry little laugh.

'So,' grunted Pierre de Gingerbeard, continuing to mould the marzipan frogs. He was obviously a genius. Not only was he able to create tiny miracles

130

with his thick, stubby fingers, he had the right sort of accent.

'So. We are rrrrelated. We are cuzains, twenty-fourrr times rrremoved. And you must be zat nasty leetle weetch keed 'oo used to pull my beard. Ze one 'oo sends me cheap Chreestmas carrrds and drops 'ints about 'ow much you would like a free puddeeeng, oui?'

'Mmmmm,' said Sharkadder uncomfortably, with a sideways look at Pongwiffy.

'Hum. Well, Cuzain Sharkaddaire. To what do I owe ze honaire of zees veesit? You are steel 'oping for a puddeeeeng? Or 'ave you come to sponge a sponge, huh?'

'No, not a sponge,' began Pongwiffy.

Sharkadder interrupted. 'Sssh, Pong. He's my relative. No, not a sponge, Cousin Gingerbeard. A Cake. A Very Special Cake, actually. And we've got the money to pay for it. It's for Grandwitch Sourmuddle, you see. It's her two-hundredth birthday soon, and she's going to retire. We hope.'

'A two-hundredth birthday cake, you say?' Pierre de Gingerbeard looked thoughtful. 'Now, one of zose I 'ave not made een yearrrs. 'Ow beeg you want zees cake?'

131

'Oh, big. Ever so big. It's got to be special, you see.'

'Uh-huh. A beeg, reech fruit cake, oui? Weez thick yellow marzipan and snowy white iceeng, decorrated weez leetle weetch 'ats, and a beeg pink ribbon, and candles and beautiful writing saying 'appy birthday, oui?'

'That's what we had in mind, yes.'

Pierre de Gingerbeard closed his eyes and seemed to go into a trance. Pongwiffy just had time to snatch a box of frogs and a couple of doughnuts from a passing tray and shove them under her hat before his eyes snapped open again.

'Such a cake only Pierre de Gingerbeard can make,' roared the genius, fists clenched above his head. 'I weel crreate zees cake for you, Cuzain Sharkaddaire, not because you are my cuzain twenty-four times rremoved, but because I adore to make two-hundredth birthday cakes, and I don't get ze chance often. Zees cake, Cuzain Sharkaddaire . . .' he paused for effect. 'Zees Cake Weel Be My Mastairepiece!'

A week later, and the day before Sourmuddle's party, Pongwiffy and Sharkadder were again in the

Gingerbeard Kitchens, staring in awed wonder as Pierre de Gingerbeard unveiled the masterpiece.

'Voilà!' said Pierre de Gingerbeard. 'Get a load of zat, zen!'

Pongwiffy and Sharkadder gaped at the creation, and broke into spontaneous applause. It was wonderful. It stood in all its glory on a silver platter, big as a dustbin lid, mouth-wateringly magnificent, truly the Cake of All Cakes.

Think of that cake you once saw in a baker's window, the one you drooled over for hours before being dragged off home and made to eat your cauliflower. Now forget it. Compared to Sourmuddle's Cake, that cake of your dreams is the sort of thing you could whip up out of a packet in half an hour.

The icing alone on this Cake would put the snowy wastes of Greenland to shame, so dazzling was its whiteness. The sides were decorated with fine trelliswork with never a drip, blob or wobble. Two hundred little sugar broomsticks were positioned around the edge, and two hundred small black candles were placed cleverly on the top, surrounding the piped words **happy birthday sourmuddle, two hundred glorious years**. Two hundred tiny witch hats had been cunningly fitted on as well, and a huge pink bow added the final touch. What a cake!

'Wow!' breathed Pongwiffy and Sharkadder together. 'Wow!'

'Eet ees, as you say, wow,' agreed Pierre de Gingerbeard, wiping away tears of emotion. 'Ees work of art.'

'Cousin Gingerbeard, you're a genius,' crowed Sharkadder. 'There's only one thing that bothers me.'

'I know what you're going to say, Sharky,' agreed Pongwiffy. 'How are we going to get it home?'

'No. How much discount do I get? Seeing as I'm family.'

In the end, they got it home by Magic. Struggling down the mountain with the huge Cake was a daunting prospect, as the sun was setting and shortly it would be dark. Delivery seemed out of the question, as immediately after Sharkadder's query about discount, Pierre de Gingerbeard had passed out. Probably sheer creative exhaustion. Anyway, right now he was being carted off to bed on the only stretcher large enough to bear The Cake. It would seem rather ungrateful to insist that he be tipped off.

Magic had to be the answer. The trouble was, their Wands had been confiscated. They both racked their brains for an old spell which didn't need one in order to work. Pongwiffy, after much thought, finally came up with an ancient, dimly remembered Spell of Transport.

'Are you sure it'll work?' said Sharkadder dubiously. 'I don't trust those old spells. Unreliable. And are you sure you can get it right?'

'Positive. I learnt it at school. You never forget what you learn at school. Now, where do we want to keep The Cake?'

'I don't know. Somewhere safe. We don't want anyone to see it before tomorrow night, else it'll spoil the surprise.'

'What about my garden shed?' suggested Pongwiffy. 'It's got a big padlock, and no one'll think of looking there. And I'll be nearby to guard it.'

You didn't know Pongwiffy had a garden shed, did you? Well, she does. She uses it to grow toadstools from seed, and sometimes locks the Broom in it when it gets on her nerves.

'Hmm. All right,' agreed Sharkadder. 'You're sure it'll be safe?'

'I'm sure. Right, here goes. How did that spell go again? Oh yes, I remember . . .'

'Look, if your spell harms so much as one crumb of that Cake . . .' threatened Sharkadder.

'It won't, it won't. I know it now. Listen, you might learn something.

> Currents of the wind, now take
> To my shed this currant cake,
> Take it steady, take it slow,
> One two three and off you go.'

'Hey! Look at that — it's working. See? I told you.'

Sure enough, The Cake rose off the ground, wobbled a bit, then, very slowly and jerkily, gained in height until it was on a level with the treetops. Pongwiffy and Sharkadder watched it, squinting their eyes against the setting sun.

'It's slow all right, I'll grant you that,' said Sharkadder, pulling worriedly at her nose. 'I'm not so sure about steady, though.'

'It'll get there,' said Pongwiffy, watching The Cake lose height, gain it, lose it again, wobble off in totally the wrong direction, wobble back again, hesitate, narrowly avoid a head-on collision with a surprised eagle, dither uncertainly, then finally drift off to vanish behind a peak. 'I think.'

CHAPTER NINE
Thieves

Now, this happened on a Tuesday. Remember the significant thing about Tuesday? It's the *Goblins' Hunting Night*! They were plodding back to their cave, trying hard to look forward to their supper, which was last night's warmed-up salt-flavoured water because, as usual, they hadn't succeeded in catching anything.

Well, let's be fair and give credit where it's due. Young Sproggit, at great risk to himself, had at one point made a flying tackle and brought a small glow-worm to its knees. But they all agreed that it was too small to divide satisfactorily into seven bits, and wasn't worth the trouble of carrying all the way home. So Sproggit let it go again.

Apart from that brief drama, the hunt had followed its usual pattern of checking empty traps, crashing around and bumping into trees, losing each other, falling into swamps and ditches, trying to talk like carrots in case rabbits were listening, and holding their hunting bags wide open in the hope that something might jump in. Nothing did, of course. It never does. You'd think they'd learn.

They were so fed up, they almost started fighting then and there – but agreed that perhaps they should wait until they got home, otherwise there would be nothing to do until they drank the warmed-up, salt-flavoured water at midnight – traditionally the Goblins' supper time. It was a silly Tradition, as they were always starving long before then – but all Goblin Traditions are silly, as we know. Of course, nobody thought of moving supper time forward by an hour or so. That's Goblins for you.

Anyway. Home the Goblins were trudging, sulky and defeated, not even bothering to sing. Most had their bobble hats firmly pulled down over their faces as protection against bumping into trees. They couldn't see the trees, of course, because their hats were over their faces.

One, however, was hatless, having caught a loose thread on an overhanging branch the minute he had left the cave that evening. The hat had gradually unravelled during the course of the hunt, and although his brains seemed a little chillier than usual, he noticed nothing particularly out of the ordinary until somebody pointed out his bare head and the line of wool trailing all over the Wood, tying up the trees in a sort of gigantic cat's cradle.

The bare-headed Goblin was looking up at the moon, wondering if it was indeed made of cheese, and if so, was it the ripe, round, smelly sort or the kind that comes in thin slices? It couldn't be the sort that came in little triangles, for the shape was all wrong. Though, come to think of it, so was the shape of the thin slices . . .

You will gather from this that the hatless Goblin who was looking up at the moon was incredibly stupid. He was also incredibly big. Got it? Yes, it was our old friend Plugugly, and because he leads such a dull life with those brains of his, it seems only fair to let him be the first to spot the flying Cake.

'Derrrrrr . . .' he croaked, eyes bulging, nudging everyone furiously and pointing upward. 'Will you look at dat! Dat's a flying cup, dat is!'

'Saucer, you mean,' said young Sproggit cockily. 'The saucer's what goes under the cup, see, to catch the drips. The cup's what you drink out of.'

'Yer?' said Plugugly wonderingly. ''Sfunny, I always does it de udder way round.'

Silence fell as the Goblins watched The Cake. It was acting rather strangely, zigzagging across the sky, plummeting down, zooming up high, obviously unsure of where it was going.

' 'Snorra saucer, anyway,' remarked Hog, adding wisely, 'You kin tell. Too fat fer a saucer.'

'He's right,' agreed Slopbucket. 'But if issnorra saucer, warrisit?'

'Issa UFO, that's what,' said Eyesore.

'Wassat?'

'I dunno, do I? Unattractive Female Ostrich?'

'Nah, 'snotta *nostrich*. Can't fly, kin they?'

'You got any better ideas?'

'Yer, issa spaceship, dat's worritiz. 'N' iss gonna land, an' norrible ugly little green fings is gonner come out and take over de world!'

'Per'aps we'd better run fer it, then.'

'Nah. 'Old yer ground. Can't be uglier than us, kin they?'

The Cake was hovering directly over their heads. They watched it a moment longer, then Plugugly cleared his throat.

'Know what I fink dat is? I fink dat's A Cake. An' if issa Cake, I fink we should foller it an' see where it lands, an' den . . . an' den steal it, yer, steal it, an' den . . . an' den . . .' Plugugly's brains got in a knot at that point, but the Goblins caught his drift.

'Yer! Eat it! Her her her, eat it! Hooray!' they yelled, throwing their hats in the air and kicking each other excitedly. Above them, The Cake suddenly remembered where it was going and floated off again, so the Goblins hastily got into hunting formation and tiptoed after it with much uncouth bellowing and disgustingly greedy howls.

Now, Pongwiffy's Spell of Transport had ordered the air currents to take The Cake to her garden shed. It was an old, creaky, inefficient sort of spell which is hardly ever used these days. Wands are so much better, in the way that calculators are generally more fast and reliable than sums worked out in yellow crayon on the back of an old envelope.

The Magic controlling the air currents was

primitive Magic, the sort of Magic that couldn't really cope with unexpected circumstances. Like the shed being locked.

These unreliable air currents, having taken The Cake around the air equivalent of winding country lanes instead of straight as the crow flies, finally got it to Pongwiffy's shed. The large padlock on the door was a major technical hitch, and they had no idea how to cope with it. They therefore simply deposited their burden gently in Pongwiffy's prize nettle patch and blew away, eager to get back and play amongst the pine trees on the mountain.

All would have been well if Pongwiffy had come straight home. She would most probably have arrived before The Cake, and the shed would have been unlocked and everything would have been hunky-dory. However, it didn't happen that way.

Halfway home, she suffered a rather unpleasant attack of airsickness (brought on, no doubt, by too many marzipan frogs and stolen doughnuts) and had to order the Broom to make an emergency landing on a village green. There she drank a great deal of water from the pump, and lay around moaning feebly and holding her stomach while the Broom hung above and struck up a conversation with a nearby lawnmower.

Sharkadder, who had also pinched some marzipan frogs but had the will power to save them for later, flew straight home, lulled into a false sense of security by Pongwiffy's assurances that the spell would work and that anyway, she (Pongwiffy) would definitely arrive back before The Cake did, and would make absolutely sure it was safely settled down for the night, so no worries, no problems, etc., etc.

Of course, Sharkadder should have worried. If, instead of climbing into her dressing gown and slapping on several layers of bedtime cleansing mud, she had gone to check that both The Cake and Pongwiffy had arrived back, The Cake would never have been stolen by Goblins.

But she didn't. So it was.

'I beg your pardon? For one moment there, I thought you said The Cake had been stolen, ha ha ha,' said Sharkadder, standing at her door in her nightcap, face crisp with dried cleansing mud, chin flaked with green marzipan, clutching a mug of cocoa, obviously just about to get into bed.

'I did! It has been! I came right over, Sharky, quick as I could,' babbled poor Pongwiffy. 'It wasn't my fault,' she added.

'Stolen? You mean . . . *stolen?*' said Sharkadder stupidly, unable to take it in.

'Yes! Yes! By Goblins!'

'Goblins? If this is a joke . . .'

'No! No joke. It's true.'

'Goblins have stolen The Cake? Sourmuddle's Birthday Cake? *Cousin Gingerbeard's Masterpiece?*'

'Yes, I keep *saying*. I know it was Goblins, because I've got evidence. Look!' Pongwiffy thrust a filthy bobble hat under Sharkadder's nose.

'See? One of them must have dropped it. The Cake got back all right – my nettle patch is full of icing sugar crumbs. But it couldn't get into the shed because of the padlock. So the Goblins must have seen it sitting there in the garden. We're lucky they didn't eat it on the spot, but I know they didn't because there's this trail of crumbs leading to their cave. Besides, they never eat out. So they must have it in there, and they'll start eating it on the first stroke of midnight. That's their supper time. Oh, Sharky, what are we going to do?'

Sharkadder decided then and there what she

was going to do. Without any hesitation, she fainted clean away, right on the doorstep. It wasn't much help.

Pongwiffy debated whether to revive her, and decided against it. When Sharkadder came round she would doubtless start shouting and saying I-told-you-so and breaking friends and things like that. Best to leave her there and try to get The Cake back by herself. How, badness only knew – but try she would. After all, one Witch, even without her Wand, is more than a match for a Gaggle of Goblins. Especially if that Witch is our Pong.

The Goblins, meanwhile, could hardly believe their luck. After weeks of coming home with nothing more than severe headaches, they had at last succeeded in tracking down and capturing An Entire Cake. What's more, it was a Witch's Birthday Cake! The Goblins couldn't read the writing on the top, but the icing sugar Broomsticks and witch hats were clues which even they could understand. There were a lot of candles too, which meant that the birthday Witch was probably quite old. The Goblins could only count up to two, but all agreed that there were lots more than that.

Lardo suggested that perhaps it was that ol' Pongwiffy's Birthday Cake, as it had been captured whilst sitting in her front garden. This made them even more gleeful. What a laugh, to eat that ol' Pongwiffy's Birthday Cake – wouldn't she be furious, har har har.

All this jollity passed the time rather pleasantly, until it was five minutes to midnight. They were sitting in a circle on the floor, surrounding the wonderful Cake which was set on a low rock at the cave centre. Sproggit, the official timekeeper, being the only one with a watch, commenced the countdown. This was a particularly pointless Tradition, as his watch only told the time in days and both the hands were missing. It wasn't necessary anyway, as Goblins always know when it's midnight because their empty stomachs begin to itch. They call it the Itching Hour.

Anyway. Sproggit was doing the countdown, Slopbucket was sharpening the cake knife, and the air was filled with the horrible drooling, slobbering, lipsmacking, stomach-scratching sounds which precede every Goblin meal.

'Fifty-nine seconds . . .' intoned Sproggit. 'Fiftyten seconds . . . er . . . forty-twelve . . .'

And then it happened. Of all inconvenient things, there came a brisk knocking at the front door – or front boulder, if you want to be fussy.

The Goblins looked at each other in alarm. Supposing it was that old Pongwiffy, come to claim back The Cake? They clutched each other fearfully as Plugugly went to answer the boulder, which was *his* official job.

When he came back again, he wasn't alone. With him was a Mysterious Stranger, wearing clothing that was rather Spanish in style and carrying a wicker basket containing bunches of heather. She looked very exotic.

Around her head was tied a spotted head-scarf. She wore a blouse with big puffy sleeves, a purple shawl, a swirly red skirt and lots of jangling jewellery, including huge hoop earrings and a pendant in the shape of a crystal ball. She also wore a large pair of sunglasses, which added to the air of mystery.

We know who it is, don't we? We're not stupid like the Goblins. We'd know Pongwiffy anywhere, if only by her smell. Mind you, she had done rather a good job with her disguise. The only thing which

148

rather spoilt the overall effect was her boots, but that wasn't her fault. When she tried taking them off, Hugo had insisted she put them back on again *immediately*. So the disguise isn't perfect in every detail. But if you ever caught a whiff of Pongwiffy's exposed feet, you too would feel it was a risk worth taking.

'Good evening, kind sirs!' trilled Pongwiffy, rattling a pair of castanets. 'Buy a few pegs from the mysterious fortune teller. Cross my palm with silver, flamenco dancing a speciality, get your lucky heather here! Anyone want their fortune told?'

'It'd better be short,' said Plugugly. ' 'Cos we is 'avin' our supper.'

'So I see, sir, so I see. And what a lovely Cake that is, sir.'

'Never mind dat. Warrabout my fortune?'

'Patience, sir, patience. Don't want to bring a nasty curse down upon your head, do you? Oh, but what a lucky face you have, sir! See that wart, right there on your nose? That means a journey, sir, a long journey over water. And that pimple on your neck stands for a tall stranger who will bring you good luck.'

'Yer? Gerraway!' said Plugugly, pleased.

'Now, let me see your hand.' Pongwiffy casually placed her basket on the floor and inspected Plugugly's filthy paw, bracelets jangling.

'Aha! I thought so. It's all here, you know. Plain as can be. You're going to meet a beautiful She-Goblin with long matted hair like old rope and little red piggy eyes. She'll fall in love with you at first sight.'

'Cor! Just my type. 'Ear dat, you lot?'

'And what's more, I see a wedding, with much dancing and delicious things to eat. And what's this? Oho! Oh ho ho ho! I see six – no, seven little baby Goblins, bald they are, climbing all over you, sir, and calling you Daddy.'

'Yer? You can really see all dat?' said Plugugly, his eyes misting over.

'Clear as day. It's all here, on your love line. In fact, one's being sick down your shirt right now.'

Pongwiffy's performance was going down rather well, much to her relief. The other Goblins in the cave had torn their eyes away from The Cake, and were listening intently, mouths open.

'And their names,' continued Pongwiffy, 'their names are written here as well. Skwawk, Shreek, Grizzle, Boo, Hoo, and – er – Plop.' That only came to six, of course, but the Goblins couldn't count, so it didn't matter.

'My little boys,' wept Plugugly emotionally. 'What lovely names!'

'They're girls actually,' Pongwiffy corrected him. 'Except for Plop.'

'Even better. I'll buy dem pink frilly dresses ter go wiv dere bovver boots. An' a blue Goblin-gro fer Plop.'

By now, the Goblins were all beginning to crowd around, eager to hear the rest of Plugugly's fortune and dying to have their own hands read. So intent werc they at being first in the queue, they didn't notice the small Hamster, disguised as a bunch of heather, slip out of the basket, scuttle towards The Cake, swing himself up and duck out of sight in the folds of the pink bow.

'What else, fortune teller?' Plugugly was saying. 'Anyfin' else?'

'That's all I see on your love line. Now, let's look at your life line, shall we? Wait a minute. Where is it? You haven't got one!'

'Eh?'

'I don't believe it, everyone has a life line – ah, here it is. But it's so short! I've never seen one as short as this. According to this line, your life is about to end very, very soon.'

'What? How soon?' Plugugly had gone very pale, and his hand trembled.

'According to this, in about two minutes.'

'What? 'Ang on, you muster made a mistake.'

'Oh sir, sir, the lines don't lie! There's going to be a dreadful catastrophe. It's written quite plainly on your palm. Hold your hands up, everyone, quick! Yes, yes, it's as I thought! You've all got short life lines! There's going to be a disaster. Oh, doom, doom. Doom and woe!'

'What? What's going to happen?' quavered the alarmed Goblins.

'What about my little girls?' wailed Plugugly. 'And Plop? What about Plop?'

'Yes, it's very unfortunate, I do agree,' said Pongwiffy, shaking her head with a worried look. 'But disaster's at hand, I feel sure of that. The question is, what sort of disaster? Flood? Fire? Plague? Maddened Pandas? Killer Ladybirds? Blood-Crazed Bunny Rabbits? Could be anything – hard to say. Of course, the most likely thing is a bomb.'

'What did she say? A what?' gibbered the Goblins,

eyes bulging.

'A bomb. I've just got this feeling that there's a bomb somewhere in this cave, and any minute now it's going to go off! We have to find it – there's not a minute to lose! Think, kind sirs, think, I beg of you! Has anything been brought into this cave recently which is . . . *big enough to hide a bomb*?'

Pongwiffy stared pointedly at The Cake, but the Goblins merely shrugged, looked frightened and gnawed their fingernails. The word Bomb had clearly sent them into a state of shock, and their brains had jammed. She saw she would have to spell it out even more clearly.

'Now, let's not panic. We must remain calm. We are looking for a bomb. A bomb in disguise, a cleverly hidden bomb. Now, what do bombs do? Think!'

The Goblins looked blank. Bombs, bombs. What did bombs do again? They knew it was something awful, it was on the tip of their tongues but they just couldn't think . . .

'Why, they tick, of course! Let's all be very quiet for a moment, and see if we can hear ticking.' There was an instant silence. Then:

'Teek,' went The Cake, dead on cue. 'Teek, teek,

teek, teek . . .'

'The Cake!' howled Pongwiffy, pointing a trembling finger. 'There's a bomb in The Cake! It's going to go off!'

That was it! That's what bombs do! They go off! Seven Goblin mouths opened and let out seven Goblin howls. And before you could say bobble hat, the cave was deserted!

'You see? Told you it'd work,' said Pongwiffy to Hugo as the screaming faded away in the distance. 'Nothing to it. Operation Cake Rescue successful. At ease, Sergeant.'

'Not quite,' said Hugo, emerging from his hiding place and pulling heather from his ears. 'Ve 'asn't got it 'ome yet.'

'Elementary, my dear Hugo. I shall use a Rolling Spell. I don't trust that Spell of Transport.'

'A Rollink Spell?'

'Yes, I learnt it in school. How did it go again? Oh yes, I know. Stand back, Hugo. How often do I have to tell you I need room when I cast spells? Right.

Rolling drums and rolling pins,
Rolls of fat make double chins,

Rock and roll is here to stay,
Make this Cake now roll away!'

And after a moment, to their great relief, The Cake heaved, shuddered, shifted sideways, crawled off the silver platter and plopped on to the floor in a shower of crumbs. Several witch hats and Broomsticks became unstuck in the process, but at least the spell was working. Once on the floor, it flipped over on its side and began to roll towards the cave's exit. Pongwiffy and Hugo scurried after it and emerged into the moonlit night just in time to see it go rolling briskly down the slope, looking rather like a giant runaway junior aspirin.

'Some of ze decorations, see, zey fall! Make it go slower,' squeaked Hugo as they scrambled down after it, tripping over hidden roots and inconveniently placed boulders.

'Slower, Cake!' howled Pongwiffy, falling headlong over a tree stump and grazing her knees quite badly. 'Oh bother, I've lost my scarf! I said slower, Cake!'

The Cake didn't seem to be slowing down at all. If anything, it was gaining speed. Before Pongwiffy had picked herself up, it had reached the bottom of

155

the hill and was already halfway up another one.

'Ve 'ave to let it go,' gasped Hugo, wringing sweat from his whiskers. 'Ve never catch it now.'

'Oh no? That's what you think!' Pongwiffy's voice took on that deep, ringing tone that actors always use when making an important speech. She clenched her fist in the air as well. All things considered, she really looked quite good. A pity her knee was bleeding, though.

'I shall follow this Cake wherever it goes!' she thundered. 'Let no one stand in my way! However long it takes, however far the path may lead, even to the ends of the earth, I shall follow! The way may be long and hard, fraught with dangers and perils, but I shall follow! The rivers may be deep and the mountains high . . .'

There was a great deal more of the same, but that's enough for you to get the idea. And this seems a rather good moment for us to leave. Let's move on to exactly twenty-four and a half hours later. We're allowed to do that if we want. We should spend a bit of time with Sourmuddle. After all, she is two hundred years old.

CHAPTER TEN
The party

Twenty-four and a half hours later was the night of Grandwitch Sourmuddle's birthday party. Of course, Sourmuddle didn't know this. She thought it was just another monthly Crag Hill Meeting. She was, however, Expecting Trouble. The whispering and giggling behind her back had become more noticeable of late, and even Snoop was nowhere to be found. Sourmuddle was totally convinced that there was treachery in the air – but she wasn't Coven Mistress for nothing. She was prepared.

She zoomed in, dismounted, parked her

Broomstick and marched into the glade. She was in full combat gear – armour-plated hat, spell-proof vest, flak rags – the lot. She was also hung about with charms, amulets, talismans, bells, books and candles. She held a Wand in one hand and a catapult in the other. She bristled with stink bombs and wishbones. Her pockets were crammed with powders and potions of every description, and she was prepared, at a moment's notice, to vanish, turn into a leopard, shrink, grow into a giantess, or anything which might be appropriate, depending on what the rebel Witches chose to throw at her. In other words, she was Ready For Action. Plot against the Coven Mistress, would they? She'd show 'em.

The Witches and their Familiars were all assembled on the hill. There was no evidence of any weapons, Sourmuddle noticed. In fact, they seemed to be wearing party rags – but this was probably all part of the plan to pull the wool over her eyes.

'Right, you lot, do your worst!' shrilled Sourmuddle, taking up a battle pose and glaring around. 'I know you've been plotting against me! I'm not stupid, you know. I'm not Grandwitch for nothing! Oh, so there you are, Snoop, you traitor. Gone over to the enemy, eh? Well, I don't need you. I don't need anyone. I . . . what are all these decorations doing?'

Suddenly, Sourmuddle became aware of the strings of gaily coloured Witch lights strung through the trees. There were paper streamers too, and lanterns. And what was this? The trestle tables were literally groaning with delicious things to eat. Jellies, little sausages on sticks, cheese straws, chocolate biscuits, ice cream, more ice cream – and not a stale spiderspread sandwich in sight! There were crackers, too, and red serviettes!

And *what was that*? *A pile of . . . presents*?

'What's going on?' quavered Sourmuddle, confused. 'What's hap—' But her voice was drowned out.

'Happy Birthday!' shouted all the Witches in unison.

Sourmuddle couldn't believe her ears. Her *birthday*? At last, it was really her BIRTHDAY? And she had thought . . . all that whispering and huddling in corners . . . she had thought they . . .

'Oh,' she whispered, a lump in her throat. 'Oh. Thank you, girls. I . . . I didn't know, you see. I . . .'

'We wanted it to be a surprise!' shouted the Witches, crowding round.

'Oh, it's that. It's that all right,' bawled Sourmuddle, mopping her eyes, feeling an absolute idiot. That she could have mistrusted her own girls! That she could have thought even for one minute that . . . oh, what a fool she had been!

She wasn't allowed to stay miserable for long, however. Gaga passed around her home-made crazy hats, which were *really* crazy, and that was the signal for the festivities to start in earnest. First, Sourmuddle had to open all the cards, which was done rather hastily because she was dying to get on to the presents. And what presents!

There was a pair of bookends in the shape of Broomsticks from Agglebag and Bagaggle. They were a bit flimsy for bookends, being made of paper, but everyone agreed that they were very clever.

Bonidle's gift was a paperweight in the shape of an old brick. Well, to be honest, it *was* an old brick, but Bonidle had tied a red ribbon round it, so it looked quite pretty for a brick.

'What a lot of trouble you've gone to, Bonidle,' said Sourmuddle happily, and Bonidle flushed with pride.

Gaga's present was a cardboard box containing some loose screws (she had plenty of those), some orange peel (fertiliser for Sourmuddle's tomato plants), an egg which ticked when shaken and which Gaga thought would hatch into a cuckoo clock, and some joke bat droppings. At least, Sourmuddle rather hoped that they *were* joke ones. At any rate, she said that she liked all the things, and couldn't wait for the cuckoo clock to hatch. Gaga was so pleased she had to rush off and hang upside-down from a tree for a bit.

Macabre's tartan hanky was a great success. Sourmuddle tried it out right away, and didn't mind a bit when her nose immediately became a riot of small red and green squares, which didn't wash off for a fortnight – Macabre's uncle again, who also dealt in dyes.

'I like it,' declared Sourmuddle, examining her tartan nose in a mirror. 'I feel it's me. Thanks, Macabre.'

Another triumph was Greymatter's book of crossword puzzles, which Greymatter had already thoughtfully filled in.

Ratsnappy's stinging nettle plant would look just perfect on her coffee table, declared Sourmuddle. And the bottle of home-made shampoo from Scrofula was just what she needed, as her dandruff had recently shown alarming signs of clearing up.

Sludgegooey's sink plunger was duly admired, as was the set of lipsticks from Sharkadder in six shades of green: Moss, Nettle, Seaweed, Mould, Bile and Scummy Pond.

Only Pongwiffy was absent, and the truth was that nobody had even noticed in the excitement. Even if they had, it was unlikely that they would have cared that much – they were all having far too good a time.

The presents had all been unwrapped and Sourmuddle was sitting, glowing with pleasure, amidst the wrapping paper, examining all her new things. Sharkadder suddenly took command. She clapped her hands and called for silence.

'Tea next!' she announced. There was a burst of clapping and loud cheers, and a surge towards the trestle tables.

'Hold it! First, a surprise. Are you ready back there?'

'Oui!' came a familiar voice from somewhere in the bushes. And from out of those bushes, you'll be astounded to hear, marched none other than Pierre de Gingerbeard – and in his wake came two more Dwarfs carrying between them a large stretcher on which was sitting: THE CAKE!

A cry of wonder went up as the Witches saw The Cake for the first time. There it sat, a great snowy mountain, every witch hat and Broomstick in place and pink bow crisply curled. The two hundred candles were alight, and it looked so beautiful, the Witches were awestruck – especially Sourmuddle, who burst into tears of gratitude. It was a moment of great drama – slightly spoilt, however, by someone who chose that exact moment to crawl into the glade from the opposite direction.

Who? Our Pong, of course – and a sorry sight she looked too. There were twigs in her hair and rips in her blouse. The hem of her skirt had come undone and trailed in the mud. She had lost both earrings, her scarf, her shawl, both castanets and twenty-three bangles. A small bedraggled Hamster limped at her side, cheek pouches sagging with exhaustion and golden fur soaked with perspiration. Both of them looked just about all in.

'I'm sorry, Sharky!' croaked Pongwiffy. 'I know you'll never forgive me, but we did our best. We've been trailing it all day, but we just couldn't catch it, could we, Hugo? Badness knows where it's gone – we've looked everywhere . . .' And then she stopped, eyes on stalks as she spotted The Cake on the stretcher. There it was, all two hundred candles blazing merrily, not a crumb out of place.

'What are you babbling about, Pongwiffy?' said Sourmuddle. 'You're late for my party. And why are you dressed as a scarecrow? It's not fancy dress, y'know. Now, stop trying to hog the limelight. This is my night, and I'm going to enjoy it. Just let me feast my eyes for one moment on That Cake. My, that's Some Cake, that is.'

'This is my cousin, Pierre de Gingerbeard, Sourmuddle. You know, the famous chef? He made

it especially for you,' said Sharkadder.

'Well, I'm very honoured, I'm sure,' said Sourmuddle, and Pierre de Gingerbeard gave a stiff little bow and said the honour was his.

'Blow out the candles,' urged the Witches when The Cake was transferred from the stretcher to the centre of the trestle table. Wiping away a tear, Sourmuddle blew out the candles as the Witches sang ten more choruses of 'Happy Birthday' and six of 'For She's a Jolly Good Fellow'. It took that long because you don't have much puff when you're two hundred.

'Hooray!' everyone cheered as the last candle flickered out. 'Cut it now, Sourmuddle!'

Sourmuddle took a sharp knife and solemnly cut the first slice.

'I now declare this tea open!' she bellowed, taking a vast bite – and with happy cries, the Witches fell upon the trestle tables and began to stuff themselves in earnest.

'Come on, Pong,' said Sharkadder kindly, going up and putting her arm around her drooping friend. 'Come and eat something before you fall down.'

'I don't understand,' muttered Pongwiffy weakly. 'Is that the same Cake?'

'Of course. Let's go and grab a slice before it's all gone.'

'But how? Why? We've been searching for it all day, but the Rolling Spell made it go too fast, you see, and we just couldn't catch up . . .'

'Rolling Spell? What, you used another of those wonky old spells of yours? That explains it.'

'Explains what?'

'Well, you see, after I came round from my faint, I flew straight to the Gingerbeard Kitchens to see if Cousin Pierre had a spare sponge or something, and we were just talking about what an idiot you were when in it rolled, just like that. A bit battered, of course, but Cousin Pierre soon repaired the damage. I suppose it's a homing cake. Like homing pigeons, you know. I'm surprised you didn't think of that. It's obvious it'd make for home. Why, what are you doing, Pong?'

'Crying,' said Pongwiffy, who was.

'Well, don't. Not at a party. Everything turned out all right in the end, didn't it? No bones broken.'

'You haven't seen my knees. I fell over at least a million times, and Hugo got stuck down a rabbit hole, and then there was the bull . . .'

'Yes, well, tell me all about it when you get your

strength back. Come on, Pong, it's a party. You love parties.' And firmly, she led Pongwiffy towards the trestle tables.

After a cup of bogwater, Pongwiffy felt a little better. After seventeen sausage rolls and four plates of trifle, she really began to perk up. By her sixth dish of ice cream, she felt ready to join in the games, and by her ninth chocolate eclair, there was no holding her back.

But if Pongwiffy enjoyed herself, you should have seen Sourmuddle. Two hundred years old she might have been, but you'd never have known it. She danced jig after jig with Pierre de Gingerbeard until he finally begged to be allowed to collapse on the spot. Then she danced a few on her own, only sitting down when Agglebag and Bagaggle's violins became so hot they couldn't play them any more.

She joined in all the party games and, owing to her incredible energy and remarkable talent for cheating, won every prize. Nobody complained, because after all, it was her birthday. Besides, everyone was busily being smarmy in the hopes that they might be chosen as Grandwitch. So they smiled when Sourmuddle tripped them up and pushed them off the chairs in Musical Chairs, laughed when she blew squeakers in their faces, joined loudly in the songs about how great she was and didn't even complain when, in an excess of high spirits, she poured trifle down the back of their robes. What a time Sourmuddle had!

She was still going strong when dawn broke, and had to be forcibly strapped on to the cake stretcher and carried home, still giggling, and startling the early birds with vigorous blasts of song.

Pongwiffy, Hugo, Dudley and Sharkadder went with her, to help Snoop get her safely tucked up in bed. They tipped the Dwarfs who carried the stretcher with Pongwiffy's Magic Coin – the one which always returns to her purse ten minutes later. That was mean, but Witches are like that. The Dwarfs doffed their caps and trudged off back to Crag Hill again, where their master lay snoring with his head on the silver platter of cake crumbs. It took them the whole of that day to cart him back up the Misty Mountain. They were the only ones who didn't enjoy the party.

It took ages to get Sourmuddle undressed and into bed because of the alarming number of weapons and Magical bits and pieces they found all over her – but finally it was done. Hugo and Dudley placed all her presents on her bedside table, so that she could look at them whilst she went to sleep.

'I don't see one from you, Pongwiffy,' Sourmuddle remarked, yawning.

'I haven't given it to you yet,' explained Pongwiffy, thinking of the gift-wrapped dustbin she had spent the last week scraping out. 'I had other things on my mind.'

'Pong helped me organise The Cake, you know,' said Sharkadder loyally. 'She's worked very hard to make your birthday a success.'

'To be sure. You all have. I never had a better time in my life.'

'I – er – I suppose you'll be thinking of retiring now,' said Pongwiffy. 'Now you're two hundred.'

'Who, me? Retire? Not on your life. Not till I'm four hundred. I've always said that. You'd better start thinking about planning my retirement party soon, you know. There's only another two hundred years to go. Goodnight.'

And with that, she blew out her bedside candle and began to snore.

There was a silence. Then:

'Oh well,' said Sharkadder with a sigh. 'Might as well go home, I suppose. I don't expect she wanted to say it in front of you.'

'Say what?' said Pongwiffy, following her out.

'Well, it's obvious she was joking. Of course she plans to retire. I expect she'll tell me in the morning.'

'Tell you what? *What?*'

'That I'm to be Grandwitch, of course. I mean, I'm the obvious choice.'

'Quite right,' growled Dudley.

'*Obvious choice? YOU?*' howled Pongwiffy. 'Hear that, Hugo? Talk about stuck-up. If anyone's going to be chosen, it'll be me. Who's got the toughest Familiar? Eh? Eh?'

'True,' chipped in Hugo.

'What's true?' snarled Dudley. 'If it weren't fer me bad back . . .'

'And who organised the Talent Contest?' howled Pongwiffy. 'And who got The Cake from the Goblins? Me, that's who.'

'Don't be ridiculous,' sneered Sharkadder. 'You need somebody with good dress sense representing the Coven. Not some smelly old tramp in a torn cardigan.'

'*Smelly old tramp . . . are you referring to me?* D'you know the first thing I'll do when I'm Grandwitch? I'll break friends with you, and have you thrown out of the Coven!' roared Pongwiffy.

'Oh ha ha ha!' jeered Sharkadder, flouncing along. 'Come on, Dudley. I don't want you associating with that Hamster. It's been badly brought up. When your back's better, you can teach it who's boss.'

' 'E can teach me now if 'e like,' snapped Hugo challengingly. 'Come on, vindbag. Vant a fight?'

'Oh, me back, me back . . .'

'Thrown out of the Coven! Thrown out of the Coven!' taunted Pongwiffy.

'Stinkpot. You stink, Pongwiffy – admit it. 'Scuse me while I put this clothes peg on my nose . . .'

And so the arguments raged on and the insults flew as they all strolled home through the early morning dew.

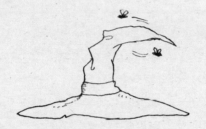

Turn the page for another
Pongwiffy adventure!

the Pongwiffy stories

The Goblins' Revenge

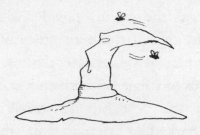

CHAPTER ONE
An Early Morning Crawler

Witch Sharkadder was sitting at her dressing table Getting Ready, and it was a serious business. It involved a great deal of preening and pouting in fly-flecked mirrors. It involved the smearing on of various horrid substances which were stored in dozens of mysterious little pots and bottles. Getting Ready needed time, concentration, and above all, quiet. Even Dead Eye Dudley, Sharkadder's Cat, knew better than to interrupt when Mistress was Getting Ready.

Sharkadder had been preparing for some time

now, and had completed the basic groundwork. All facial cracks were filled in, and every bit of her long nose was thoroughly powdered. Her eyelids were painted an evil shade of green and sprouted an alarming pair of spiderleg eyelashes. There were wild splodges of rouge on both cheeks.

Now for the best bit. The final touch. The Lipstick. Sharkadder pored over the delicious possibilities. What should it be today? Hint of Gore? Boiled Beetroot? Squashed Plum Purple? Finally she selected her favourite, Toad Green. Pursing her lips, she leaned forward and carefully . . . oh, so carefully . . . began to apply it. Then . . .

'Yoo-hoo! Shaaaaaaaarky! It's me, Pongwiffy. Can I come in?'

This cheery shout was accompanied by heavy battering at the door.

Sharkadder jumped like a scalded cat and smeared a greasy trail of Toad Green from chin to earlobe. As the familiar smell wafted in, Dead Eye Dudley peered over the edge of his basket and opened his one good eye.

'Don't let her in,' advised Dudley. 'You'll be sorry.'

It was too late. The door crashed open and Witch

Pongwiffy stood on the threshold.

'Fancy Dress!' she announced.

'Fancy what?' said Sharkadder.

'That's my latest idea for the Hallowe'en party,' explained Pongwiffy, scuttling in and slamming the door behind her. 'A Fancy Dress parade. I just had to tell you about it. I say, Sharky, there's a horrible trail of green slime on your face, did you know? I think something's just died on it. Look, I've brought you a peace offering. A lovely bunch of flowers. I'll just put them in a jug or something.'

Beaming, she produced three drooping dandelions from behind her back, thrust them under Sharkadder's pointed nose, then pushed past and started crashing about in cupboards, looking for a jug or something.

'You've got a cheek,' hissed Sharkadder, inspecting the damage in a mirror. 'Coming round here, after everything. You've got a nerve.'

'Isn't it a lovely morning?' continued Pongwiffy, pretending she hadn't heard. 'I woke up and said to Hugo, "This is just the sort of morning to go and visit my best friend."'

'Go and visit her, then,' suggested Sharkadder coldly.

'Don't be silly. I meant you, of course,' explained Pongwiffy.

'Me?' said Sharkadder indignantly. 'Your best friend? After what you called me the other night? Ha! Don't make me laugh.'

Huffily, she reached for a dirty rag and scrubbed away at the green smear.

'Did I call you something the other night?' asked Pongwiffy, sounding surprised.

'You know you did. An Over-painted Bone Bag. With A Face Like A Dead Haddock. I think that was the term.'

'Oh, that! You didn't take any notice of *that*, did you?' pooh-poohed Pongwiffy, ramming the dandelions any old how into an ancient baked bean tin. 'I didn't mean it, silly. I'd never want to insult my oldest friend. My *dearest* friend. There. Your flowers. Don't they look nice now they're arranged?'

'No,' Sharkadder said frostily. 'They don't. I wasn't born yesterday, Pongwiffy. You want something, don't you?'

'Certainly not. I just want to make up, that's all. Look, I apologise. Sorry sorry sorry. There. Now, I'll just pop the kettle on, and we'll have a nice cup of bogwater and a chat, eh? I've missed you, you know, Sharky. I always do when we're not speaking.'

Sharkadder sniffed and tossed her hair sullenly. But she was beginning to come round. You could tell.

'I can't wait to tell you all my news,' said Pongwiffy, rattling the cups around. 'I've been terribly busy working on a brilliant new spell. Guess what? The rubbish is safe! I've finally solved my security problems. Want to know how?'

'Not really,' said Sharkadder. She didn't share her friend's enthusiasm for smelly old rubbish. But then, she wasn't Official Dumpkeeper. Pongwiffy was, and she really loved her work. The Dump was her pride and joy. Her hovel, Number One, Dump Edge, stood right on the edge of it.

'I'll tell you anyway,' said Pongwiffy. 'I've invented this amazing magical Wall Of Smell. It's an invisible wall that goes all the way round The Dump. It's so disgusting that nobody can get anywhere near it without a special magic formula which only I know. So yah boo sucks to the raiding parties! They won't get as much as a chair leg this year, I promise you. The famous Witches' Hallowe'en Bonfire will reach even dizzier heights!

Aren't I a rotten old spoilsport?'

'You certainly are,' agreed Sharkadder.

'When The Dump's in danger, I'll stick at nothing,' announced Pongwiffy. 'I'm not sharing my rubbish with any old Troll, Spook or Banshee. That's Witch rubbish, that is, and it's going on the Witch bonfire, or my name's not Pongwiffy.'

Pongwiffy was rightfully proud of her dump. It had a fine reputation. It had been voted Top of the Tips for three years running. That, of course, made it a prime target for raids. Every year, on the run-up to Hallowe'en, it was regularly invaded by all sorts of unsavoury types, looking for choice items to sling on their Hallowe'en bonfires.

At Hallowe'en, there are a lot of parties going on, and a great big bonfire is a MUST. The fact remains, however, that the Witches' Hallowe'en blaze is far and away the best. It's the envy of all, and Pongwiffy likes to keep it that way by all the foul means at her disposal. On the run-up to Hallowe'en, therefore, Dump Security becomes A1 Priority. It suddenly bristles with *NO TERSPASSERS* and *PRIVIT KIPPOWT* signs. It is patrolled regularly by both Pongwiffy herself and a small, fierce Hamster who goes for the ankles. That's fair enough so far.

But using Magic?

That was cheating.

'It's cheating,' said Sharkadder. 'The Skeletons won't like it. Neither will the Ghouls. I can't see the Werewolves taking it lying down. There'll be trouble, mark my words.'

'Nothing I can't handle,' said Pongwiffy confidently. 'Hey, I can't wait for tonight's Meeting, can you? We're discussing the party, remember? And, Sharky! *Guess whose turn it is to organise it this year?* Mine! And you know what a great organiser I am. I tell you, Sharky, this party will pass into legend. Pong's Great Hallowe'en Party! No, correction. Pongwiffy *and Sharkadder's* Great Hallowe'en Party. Because I want you to help me. You will, won't you? Oh, say you will!'

Sharkadder was tempted. Despite herself, she had missed Pongwiffy. Dead Eye Dudley gave a loud warning cough.

'Listen,' continued Pongwiffy. 'I found this wonderful book in the rubbish tip. It's called *How To Make Your Party Swing*. That's where I got the fancy dress idea. Sharky, I'm going to make this party swing so high it'll overbalance altogether. I mean, let's face it, the rest of the Coven wouldn't know a swinging party if it swung back and bashed 'em in the chops. They need up to date sort of Witches like you and me. I'm going to put forward my revolutionary suggestions at the Meeting tonight. I bet everyone's dead impressed. No one's ever thought of fancy dress before. Probably never even *heard* of it, ha ha . . .'

Prattling away, Pongwiffy made a confident beeline for the cupboard and got out Sharkadder's biscuit tin, which was clearly marked 'Private'. She poked around and ate the last chocolate one. She went to Sharkadder's special cake tin and cut herself a huge slice of the fungus sponge which Sharkadder was saving for tea. She found Sharkadder's secret hoard of gingerbread frogs and helped herself to nine. Dudley stationed himself before his tins of Sharkomeat and prepared to fight to the death.

'Make yourself at home,' said Sharkadder, heavily sarcastic. She should have thrown Pongwiffy out then and there, of course, but her curiosity was aroused.

'Thanks, I will.' Pongwiffy bustled over to the table with a piled plate and two cups of hot, strong bogwater. She stuffed three gingerbread frogs into her mouth, added five sugars to her own cup, and stirred it with the nearest thing to hand, which happened to be Dudley's flea comb. She slumped into a chair, took a huge slurp, wiped her mouth with the sleeve of her old cardigan, placed her boots on the table and sighed with pleasure. Her table manners really were disgraceful. Sharkadder chose to ignore them.

'What's fancy dress, then?' asked Sharkadder despite herself.

'Oh, don't you know? I thought everyone did. Well, it's where you dress up as something and parade around. And the best costume wins first prize. A hamper, I thought, from Swallow and Riskit. You just can't beat their cold skunk pie.'

'What – you mean – not wear rags?' said Shark-adder slowly. This really was a novel idea. 'Not the hat, or the cloak, or anything?'

'Nope. *Costumes*,' explained Pongwiffy, spraying sponge everywhere as she talked. 'You know. Pirates. Clowns. Scarecrows. Cinderella with her Broom. Where's *your* Broom, by the way? I haven't seen it all morning.'

'So? It's around,' said Sharkadder, suddenly suspicious. It wasn't like Pongwiffy to enquire about an absent Broomstick. 'Why?'

'Well, actually, Sharky, I've come to ask you a little favour. I have a slight problem. It's my Broom. It's lost. It's been missing since yesterday. I can't find it anywhere. I was wondering if there's any chance of a lift to Crag Hill tonight . . .'

But she didn't finish.

'I knew it!' howled Sharkadder, enraged. 'Hear that, Dudley? I *knew* she wouldn't come crawling round here unless she wanted something!'

'I told ye,' said Dudley. 'I warned ye.'

'But Sharky! I've simply *got* to be there. We're planning the *Party*,' wailed Pongwiffy. 'Surely you don't begrudge your best friend a ride on your mangy Broomstick?'

'Yes,' said Sharkadder. 'I do. And you know how Dudley feels about Hugo. How do you feel about sharing our Broom with Pongwiffy's nasty little Hamster, Duddles, darling? Be honest.'

Dudley spat on the floor.

'You see?' said Sharkadder.

'Ah Sharky, please!' wheedled Pongwiffy. 'Be reasonable. I can't possibly walk to Crag Hill. It's miles! Besides, if I don't come, I won't be able to see what you're wearing. And you always look so nice on these occasions.'

'True,' said Sharkadder, tossing her hair. She loved a compliment. 'I am rather eye-catching, aren't I?'

'You are, you certainly are. You're the most fashionable Witch in the Coven by miles. That's why I want YOU to judge the Fancy Dress parade. Oh, please say you'll take me. Do.'

'Wellllll . . .'

'Don't,' warned Dudley. ''Er called ye a haddock, remember? Don't.'

'Shut up, Dudley,' said Pongwiffy. 'This is a private conversation between Witches and nothing to do with you. What d'you say, Sharky?'

But Sharkadder never got the chance to say anything, because right at that moment the door burst open with an almighty crash!

CHAPTER TWO
stick warp

There, poised on the threshold, was Pongwiffy's missing Broomstick. It was as white as a sheet, which was unusual, because it was normally a healthy mahogany. It swept in and made for the nearest dark corner. Once there it sagged against the wall breathing hard, obviously terribly agitated.

'Badness gracious me,' exclaimed Sharkadder. 'Whatever next!'

'Aha! So there you are!' snapped Pongwiffy sternly. 'I've been looking for you everywhere, you idiot. What d'you think you're up to, barging in here like that? Bad Broom! Go outside again, and come in properly.'

The Broom cowered pathetically.

'What's wrong with it?' asked Sharkadder, poking it curiously with a long, bony finger. 'Why isn't it obeying you? Brooms are supposed to obey.'

'How should I know? It's not usually like this. Stand up straight, Broom, and do as you're told, or it's the axe for you.'

There was a clonk, and the Broom promptly passed out on the floor.

'It's fainted,' remarked Sharkadder. She poked it with her foot. 'It must have been what you said about the axe.'

'Funny,' said Pongwiffy, dousing the Broom with tepid bogwater. 'It can usually take a joke.'

The Broom sneezed, spluttered, and attempted to rise.

'Get up, you. Chop chop!' ordered Pongwiffy. Which was the worst thing she could have said, because the Broom swooned again.

'Oh, frog warts! It's passed out again. I wonder what's wrong with it? If only it could tell me.'

(It's a funny thing about Broomsticks. They can understand English but they can't speak it. That's because they speak only Wood. Wood is a highly specialised language in which the Brooms have dull wooden conversations about the problems of getting into corners and the discomfort of flying head first into a north wind. To us and the Witches it just sounds like a lot of rustling.)

'It's probably just a touch of stick warp,' said Sharkadder. She was feeling smug. Her Broom was better quality than Pongwiffy's and never gave any trouble. 'Why don't you just ask it? Try casting that Language Spell. You know, that one we learnt at school. How's it go? *Zithery zithery zoom, I want to speak to my Broom.* You know. That one.'

'No fear,' said Pongwiffy. 'I tried it once, out of curiosity. Terrible experience. Take my advice, never try talking Wood. Horrible side effects. Splinters in the mouth. Shocking taste of sawdust. Besides, the effects last for ages. It's not just limited to Brooms, you know. You can understand anything wooden. Who wants to know what dreary old shed doors and dull floorboards and stodgy old trees are yapping on about for weeks on end? I tell you, I nearly died of boredom. I'd sooner be stuck in a lift with a Goblin.'

At the word 'Goblin', the Broom suddenly

193

gave a convulsive heave and reared upright. Once vertical, it tottered groggily towards the door. Pongwiffy shot her hand out and grabbed it firmly by the stick.

'Oops!' she said. 'Looks like I shouldn't have said that either.'

'What? Goblin?'

'Yes. Stop it, Broom! Steady on!'

'Goblin?' repeated Sharkadder, enjoying the effect it had on the Broom. 'Did you say Goblin? It doesn't like the word Goblin? That's interesting. *Goblin*, you say?'

'Look, do you have to keep saying that?' complained Pongwiffy, fighting for control as the Broom struggled in her grasp.

'Saying what?' enquired Sharkadder, all innocence.

'Goblin. Oh, bother! Now you've made *me* say it. Stop it, you, before I lose my temper!'

That was to the Broom, which was getting itself into a terrible state, scrabbling and straining to get away.

'This is interesting. There's a clue here,' said Sharkadder. 'Let's think for a moment. It doesn't like AXE, CHOP CHOP, and GOBLIN. That suggests to me that it's scared that GOBLINS might come after it with an AXE and CHOP IT UP! Well, I suppose they might as well, really. I mean, look at it. It's useless. Hey, Broom! There's a Goblin right behind you! Ha, ha ha!'

'Shush!' yelled Pongwiffy. 'She's joking, she's joking!' But it was too late. The Broom finally flipped. It twisted from her grasp and hurtled around the room, smashing into Sharkadder's dressing table and sending a lifetime's collection of rare beauty aids crashing down in an explosion of lurid face powders, greasy lipsticks and small bottles of gloppy stuff.

'No-o-o-o!' screeched Sharkadder. 'My make-up! Anything but that!'

'Come back here, you! Heel!' howled Pongwiffy, stamping her foot. 'Oh, my badness. It's bolting! Stop it! It's out of control!'

It certainly was. It was like a mad thing, that Broom. Not content with the murder of Sharkadder's make-up, it knocked over the hatstand, the cauldron and three chairs before skidding in a dish of Sharkomeat and landing on Dudley's tail. Dudley swore and bit it on the stick. Sharkadder looked up from the multicoloured puddles at her feet, screamed, and attempted to do the same. The Broom dodged to one side, then launched itself at the window, intent on escape.

Pongwiffy, with great presence of mind, stuck out her foot. The Broom, blind with panic, tripped over and crashed heavily to the floor. Pongwiffy leapt on top of it and got it in a firm stranglehold.

'Behave yourself!' she screeched. 'Look at the mess you've made. Sweep it up this minute, or I'll chop you into clothes pegs!'

But there was no point in any further discussion. The Broom was out for the count and no amount of bullying could do the trick.

'Now see what you've done!' Pongwiffy glared at Sharkadder accusingly. 'Look at it! Stiff as a – well, stiff as a Broomstick. I'll never be able to ride it tonight. I'm grounded! Oh, Sharky, you've got to give me a lift to the Meeting. Please!'

'No,' snarled Sharkadder, on her knees beside the ruins of her make-up. 'Never, never, never. Not in a million trillion years. Not if you beg on bended knees. Not if you cringe and crave and implore. Not after what your Broom just did.'

'Not if I buy you a brand new collection of make-up? You can choose it yourself from the catalogue. Money no object. And I'm letting you judge the Fancy Dress parade, don't forget.'

Sharkadder hesitated.

'Can I be *in* the Fancy Dress parade as well as judge it?'

'Certainly,' said Pongwiffy immediately. 'Nothing could be fairer.'

'Done,' said Sharkadder briskly. 'See you in your garden at midnight.'

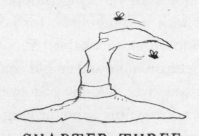

CHAPTER THREE
A Brush with Danger

By now, of course, you'll be dying to know what had happened to Pongwiffy's Broom. Why should a normally level-headed, sensible Broomstick suddenly fly off the handle like that?

Well, it had good reason. It had had a terrible shock. Something awful had happened to it.

It had been Broomnapped by Goblins!

It had happened so easily. The day before had been Thursday, and Woody was bored. (That's its name, by the way. Woody.)

Being a Witch of Dirty Habits, Pongwiffy never

199

gave it anything to do. She liked her hovel just as it was (filthy). Understandably Woody, who was an active type, got tired of being propped up in the garden shed with nothing to do for hours on end except listen to an indescribably tedious game of I Spy between a rusty rake and an old coal shovel.

Breakfast was over. Woody had swept the shed floor at least a dozen times, and the long day seemed to stretch into infinity.

'Bored,' thought Woody. 'That's what I am. Bored stiff. Fed up to the back bristles. Unamused. I must find something to do, or I'll go stark staring bonkers.'

It sneaked into the hovel and tried a bit of furtive sweeping when Pongwiffy's back was turned, but she noticed.

'Oi! You! I've told you before about that! You leave that dirt right where it is!'

Feeling fed up and generally unappreciated, Woody flounced out and went looking for Hugo, Pongwiffy's Hamster. Hugo couldn't speak Wood either, but was too kind to mind when the Broom moped around after him. However, this particular morning Hugo was nowhere to be found as he was out checking for weak points in

Pongwiffy's Wall Of Smell.

Looking for a Hamster (even one wearing a gas mask) in a rubbish dump is like looking for a tick in a Goblin's sum book. You're just wasting your time. Woody poked around a bit, then gave up.

'Now what?' it thought. It looked up. The sky was a huge, empty sweep of tempting blue, just crying out to be flown in.

'I know,' thought Woody. 'I'll go for a quiet little fly, all on my own. Brush up my flying techniques. Bit of wind in the bristles, that's the ticket.'

Now, this wasn't strictly allowed. The Witch Rule Book firmly states that Broomsticks MUST NOT fly:

1) During daylight hours.

2) Without a Witch, unless given written permission.

But if you're bored, you get tempted into doing all kinds of silly things. Just this once, Woody decided to risk it. After all, Witchway Wood was at its quietest this hour of the day. Most of the Witches would still be eating breakfast, and it was unlikely that it would be noticed. Feeling rather wicked, it did a couple of pre-flight exercises, just to get the sap moving – what Brooms call timbering up – then it took a deep breath, flexed at the base, and gave a little jump. Up it soared, over the treetops, into a nice, warm southerly wind.

'Mmmmm,' thought Woody. 'Now, this is more like it. Just what the tree surgeon ordered.'

Indeed it felt wonderfully free, up there among the clouds without Pongwiffy's bony knees jabbing into its stick.

'Wow!' thought Woody. 'It's good to be alive and a Broom today!' And it skittishly performed an easy somersault or two, then attempted a complicated triple stick loop followed by an inverted backflip. As usual it didn't quite manage it. To avoid loss of face, it chased a passing crow for a minute or so, then flipped over on its back and floated lazily on the air currents. It was enjoying itself so much, it didn't really pay any attention to where it was flying.

Where was it flying?

Directly over Goblin Territory, that's where!

Goblin Territory. That's the name given to the scrubby, stony slopes of the Lower Misty Mountains which border the edges of Witchway Wood. It's an unpopular, lonely, desolate place. There are a lot of sharp rocks up there, and it usually drizzles. Frankly, as a tourist attraction, it lacks something. Nevertheless, it is home to seven particularly stupid Goblins, who live in a cave and answer to the names of Plugugly, Stinkwart, Hog, Slopbucket, Lardo, Eyesore and Sproggit. That makes seven. One whole Gaggle.

Now, Goblins and Witches are sworn enemies, and usually prefer to live at least a thousand miles apart, so you may wonder why this particular Gaggle choose to live right next door to Witchway Wood, where so many Witches live.

Wonder no more. Plugugly, Stinkwart, Hog, Slopbucket, Lardo, Eyesore and Sproggit didn't choose. They had been dumped there by Magic, and there, much to their disgust, they had to stay.

It hadn't always been that way. In the old days they were always moving around, looking for fresh neighbours to drive mad. Until that fateful occasion when they were stupid enough to attempt squatting in a Wizard's house. The furious house-holder came back, took one look at the scandalous state of his kitchen, and cast a Spell of Banishment which whisked them away to this particular cave on this particular mountain. Right next door to Witchway Wood.

The Goblins, when they had got over

their surprise, were terribly fed up. The cave was damp and there was nothing to eat. The only place to go hunting was down in the Wood, where the Witches took great pleasure in spotting them, swatting them and booting them back to their own territory again in two whisks of a wand – a process known as 'zapping'. Not that the Goblins ever succeeded in catching anything anyway. They were much too stupid. Hungry, harrassed, hounded and frequently rained on, they had a very lean time of it.

Woody was aware of all this. Sadly, though, it was unaware that it was flying directly above Goblin Territory. It only discovered this when it was rudely knocked out of the air by a large brick.

CHAPTER FOUR
Broomnapped

The brick had been thrown by young Sproggit. Sproggit hadn't actually been aiming at Woody, although he boasted later that he had. He hadn't even noticed that there was a Broom up there. He'd just thrown a brick because he felt like it. (Throwing bricks is typically Goblinish behaviour.) So Sproggit was extremely surprised when his brick connected with Woody, bringing the poor thing crashing down out of the sky, point first on to his own foot. YEEEEOOOOOOOOOOOOOOW!

Sproggit's pained scream brought the rest of the

Gaggle pouring from their cave. When they saw what had happened, they were delirious with joy. A captured Broomstick! What luck! Even better, it was that ol' Pongwiffy's Broomstick. What a prize! What a break!

Poor Woody. They threw it about a bit, jumped on it a couple of times, then tied it up and triumphantly bore it back into the cave. Thankfully, Woody was stunned, and didn't know about any of this. Crash-landing on your sharp end from a great height is no joke.

When it came round some time later, it was horrified to find itself gagged, bound, chained and firmly padlocked to a rusty hook projecting from the wall of a dank, smelly cave. A short distance away, torches flickered on the boots, braces and bobble hats of its seven unsavoury captors, who were huddled in a conspiratorial circle, obviously plotting.

'Oh no!' groaned Woody to itself. 'Captured by Goblins! How embarrassing. Think of the shame. If the gang get to hear about this, I'll be the laughing stick of the sky. And I'm not even supposed to *be* here. Supposing Mistress finds out? I'll never live it down . . .'

Anxiously, it looked around for a means of escape. There wasn't one. The ropes were so tight, its sap was cut off. Even if it could somehow wriggle free, the front boulder was firmly shut.

'How depressing,' thought Woody. 'Alone and friendless in a cave of mad Goblins. What will become of me?'

Sick to the stick, it slumped back and reluctantly tuned in to the Goblins' conversation.

'Let's chop it up.' That was young Sproggit. 'I catched it, din I? An' I say we chops it up. Wiv an axe. Chop it up an' send it back to ol' Pongwiffy in liddle pieces. Chop chop.'

Whaaatttt?????!! Woody's sap ran cold.

'Sproggit's right,' agreed Slopbucket. 'She's gorrit comin' to 'er she 'as, that ol' Pongwiffy. Bein' so mean wiv 'er rubbish. Stickin' up that there Wall o' Smell, the ol' cheat.'

That brought a heartfelt chorus of agreement. Feelings were running high about Pongwiffy's Wall Of Smell. Raiding The Dump on the run-up to Hallowe'en was traditional. Everyone did it. Using Magic to guard it was downright mean.

'Booo!'

'Unfair!'

"'Ear! 'Ear!'

'Down wiv de Wall o' Smell.'

'That's settled then,' nodded Sproggit. 'Chop it up. Chop chop. Thas the ticket.'

''Ang about,' interrupted the biggest Goblin, nearly bursting with eagerness. His name was Plugugly, and *he had an idea*! This was a novel experience for him. 'Nar, look, listen! I gorran idear. A ransom note. See, 'ere's wot we do. We writes dis note to ol' Pongwiffy sayin' dat we taken 'er Broom 'ostage an' we demands a bag o' gold. 'Ow's dat?'

Of the two plans, Woody much preferred Plugugly's. However, to its dismay, it found itself in the minority. Everyone thought Plugugly's suggestion was terrible and said so. A ransom note? Ha! Gold? Poo! What was the point of gold? There were hardly any shops and nobody would serve Goblins anyway. But Plugugly didn't want to abandon his idea.

'Orl right! Orl right den,' he shouted above the boos. 'Ferget de gold. Let's demand sumpfin' else. Der . . . I gorrit! A free bag o' rubbish, fer our Hallowe'en bonfire. Better still, an invite to de Witches' Hallowe'en Party!'

This idea was greeted by mocking howls of

derision. Go to an old Witch party? Not on your nelly! Why, no Goblin worth his braces would be seen dead at an old Witch party. What was Plugugly thinking of? Where was his pride? Etc., etc.

'But dey always 'as a better time dan we do,' argued Plugugly stubbornly. 'Dey always got balloons. An' funny 'ats. An' stuff to eat. An' dere's dancin'. An' dat gurt big bonfire. Put ours to shame last year, dat gurt big bonfire. I mean, even wivout de Wall o' Smell, our raids always go wrong. We always gets zapped.'

The Goblins nodded and gnashed their teeth, green with envy. It was true. These Witches knew both how to protect their rubbish and how to celebrate in style. Every year, on Hallowe'en night, the Goblins had a miserable time sharing a small pot of boiled stinging nettles around a titchy, sad, damp apology for a bonfire, whilst over on Crag Hill, the Witches merrily pigged themselves on sausages and baked spuds by the light of a crackling conflagration that lit the sky for miles around. And why? Because that mean ol' Pongwiffy always got the pick of the rubbish and refused to share, that's why.

'Well, anyway, a ransom note's out,' remarked Stinkwart, who had suddenly thought of something.

'Why?'

''Cos none of us can write.' And that was true too.

'I still say we chops it up,' insisted Sproggit stubbornly. 'No one's 'ad a better idear. I mean, what else can yer do wiv a Witch's Broomstick?'

There followed a long silence, while the Goblins thought about what you could do with a Witch's Broomstick. It wasn't often they had a stroke of luck like this. They must be able to turn it to their advantage.

Over in the shadows, the subject under discussion swallowed hard and trembled.

''Ere! We can burn it,' volunteered Lardo in a flash of inspiration. 'We can make a bonfire of it, see, an' set light to it. 'Ere! We can do it on 'Allowe'en! As a sort o' protest, see. That'd really spite them Witches.'

'Hooray!' cheered Slopbucket. 'Let's do that!'

'Won't make much of a blaze,' pointed out Eyesore. 'Look 'ow thin it is. Only last a minute or two.'

Woody shuddered at the thought. It really didn't like the way the conversation was going.

'Chop it up. Chop it up,' intoned young Sproggit,

eyes glazed.

'Shame there's just the one,' said Hog. 'If we 'ad lots of 'em, there'd be a decent blaze. But we don't.'

'Chop it up. Chop it up.'

'Wait a tick,' said Plugugly suddenly. ' 'Ang about. I fink – it's comin', don't rush me – I fink I gorra plan!'

The Goblins didn't look convinced.

'No, really,' insisted Plugugly. 'I 'ave. Listen. All right, so one Broomstick duzzn't make a bonfire, I can see dat. But like Hog says, more 'n' one would! So why stick at de one? Let's capture anudder one. Den we'll capture anudder one and anudder one. See? Den, when we got all of 'em, we hides 'em so de Witches don't know where dey is.'

'Where?' asked Eyesore.

'I dunno yet, I haven't worked out all de details. Down a 'ole or sumpfin'. But you get the gen'ral idear? We takes 'em 'ostage, den we tells de Witches we'll set fire to 'em, unless dey agrees to our demands. An' if we can't fink of any demands, we'll burn 'em anyway.'

There was a pause, while the Goblins thought about this.

'See?' said Plugugly proudly. 'I said I 'ad

a plan, din I?'

'Issa plan all right,' agreed Eyesore. 'But it's full of 'oles, innit? I mean, 'ow we gonner get our 'ands on the rest of the Brooms? Eh? I mean, they ain't gonna *conveeniently* fly this way so young Sproggit 'ere can knock 'em out 'o the sky wiv bricks, are they? They're not all dozy like this one.'

Beneath its ropes, Woody nearly died of shame.

'Chop it up. Chop it up,' droned young Sproggit.

'Wait a minute,' insisted Plugugly. Success had gone to his head, and the ideas seemed to be positively bursting out. 'Dere's one time when we could do it. Tomorrer night. Coven night. We could do it while de Witches are 'avin' deir Meetin' up on Crag Hill. All de Brooms are in de Broom park, right? All togedder in de one place, see? Now what we does is we sneaks up in de dark, den we . . .'

''Arf a tick! I 'eard a noise. That there Broom's awake and snooping on our plans!' broke in Lardo. 'Come on, boys! Let's tease it. Tease break!'

Everyone welcomed the diversion. Plotting and planning was all very well, but it made the brains tired. A tease break was just what was needed.

Poor Woody. Suddenly surrounded, it tried to look proud and indifferent as the Goblins poked fun.

'Chop chop,' taunted Sproggit, pretending he had an axe. 'Chop chop.'

'Where's the matches? Somebody fetch me the matches!' bawled Lardo. Eyesore did a mocking dance, and everyone fell about laughing.

'You know, I never seen a Witch Broomstick up close before,' said Hog, wiping his eyes. 'Nuffin' special, is it? Wonder 'ow it works?'

'Dunno,' said Slopbucket. 'I s'pose there's a Magic Word or sumpfin'.'

'Sure to be,' agreed Lardo. ''Ere! Wouldn't it be good if we knew wot it was? Then we could 'ave a go at flyin' on it. Worra larf, eh?'

The Goblins looked at each other, amazed that they hadn't thought of that before. Fly on it! Of course! They slapped their knees at the thought of the laugh it would be.

''Ere!' continued Lardo. 'Let's just try it wiv a few words, eh? Never know, we might hit on the right one.'

The Goblins thought about possible words.

'Aber Cadaber.' (That was Eyesore.)

'Open Sesame Seed?' (Hog, not too confidently.)

'Eeny Meeny Miny Mo!' (Stinkwart)

'Fee fi fo fum . . .' (Slopbucket)

''Ubble bubble toil and whatsit . . .'

''Ickery Dickory Dock . . .'

Through it all, to its credit, Woody managed to maintain an aloof air of disdain. The suggestions got more and more stupid, and finally tailed off altogether.

''S no good,' remarked Eyesore. 'It ain't gonner fly, an' that's that. Tell you what, though. Seein' as it's our slave, an' it's anuvver week before we burns it, it might as well do a bit o' sweepin'. Place could do wiv it.'

'Good idear,' said Hog. 'Cut it loose, Sproggit. Plugugly, roll back that boulder a bit. We'll get a bit o' fresh air in 'ere. All this plottin's makin' my throat sore.'

Woody could hardly believe its luck. It held its breath as Sproggit fumbled with ropes and chains and padlocks, armed only with his teeth and an old fork. At the same time, Plugugly moved the front boulder to one side. Freedom was in sight.

'Right, orf yer go,' commanded Lardo. 'Let's see yer do yer stuff. Sweep!'

Woody didn't need to be told twice. It swept all right. It swept Sproggit to one side and Lardo to the other. It swept a clean path through the rest of the Goblins, cleverly avoided Plugugly, who was too big to be swept, squeezed through the narrow gap by the boulder, flung itself into the air and was off like a bat out of hell before the Goblins knew what had hit them.

Whooosh! Gone. Just like that.

Dawn was breaking as Woody flew homeward. That meant it had been in the Goblin cave all night! Oh dear. What a disaster.

As it flew, Woody's mind was a jumbled mass of seething emotions. Sheer, blessed relief, of course. That was top of the list. But after that, shame. Caught by Goblins, of all things. Why, everyone knew the Goblins never caught anything. Even a glow-worm could outwit a Goblin, because Goblins were *stupid*. Oh, idiot, idiot!

It sank further into gloom as it reflected on what would happen if the story got out. A public warning at the very least. Most probably be grounded for weeks. It would be shunned by its fellow Broomsticks. Everyone would point, and say in loud, sneery voices, 'There goes the Broom that got captured by Goblins.' Worst of all, it would have to face Pongwiffy, who would go on and on and on and on and *on*. She might even do what she was always threatening, and chop it up for clothes pegs. Oh horror!

But wait. There was a glimmer of hope. As far as it knew, there had been no witnesses. If the Goblins kept their mouths shut, there was a good chance that no one would ever know. Pongwiffy probably hadn't even missed it. Woody cheered up. Perhaps things weren't so bad after all.

But wait again. *What about the Goblins' plan?* Supposing they went through with it? Supposing they did indeed come creeping up on the defenceless Broomsticks when they were all alone in the Broom park? Just think of it. A mass Broomnapping, and all because Woody had failed to give a warning. What would happen to its friends? More important, what would happen to IT??

Woody wasn't keen to find out. Best not go to Crag Hill tomorrow night. Just as a safety precaution. Though, of course, nothing was really going to happen, was it? The Goblins would never do it, would they? They hadn't got the brains to organise something like that, had they? So there wasn't any point in mentioning it, really, was there? No, of course not.

On flew Woody, back home to Witchway Wood, determined to keep its cool. Sadly, by the time it got there, nerves had got the better of it and it had gone to pieces. Which is why we find it being dragged by a very fed up Pongwiffy back down Sharkadder's path. Insensible and in disgrace. The cause of yet another major bust-up.

CHAPTER FIVE
Ali Pali

'Come on, you lump of dead wood,' Pongwiffy growled through gritted teeth as she stomped through the Wood. 'Just you wait till I get you home.'

She was in a terrible mood. The sound of Sharkadder's slammed door was still ringing in her ears, and she felt quite queasy from eating all that humble pie. The last thing she felt like doing was dragging the comatose Broom all the way home to Number One, Dump Edge.

Autumn leaves lay thickly on the ground,

disguising various hazards, some of which were painful and some squelchy. Deep holes, sharp stones, stinging nettles, rabbit droppings – you name it, Pongwiffy fell down them, tripped over them, brushed against them or stepped in them. The Broom was not so much heavy as awkward. It got tangled in scratchy bushes and wedged in tree roots. It trailed through boggy puddles. It was a liability.

Squelch! More droppings. Haggis ones, most likely.

'Oh, badness!' Pongwiffy screeched to the Broom, at the end of her tether. 'I've had enough of this! I'm going to leave you here to rot, that's what I'm going to do!'

And she just might have done it too. But, right at that moment, there was an interesting turn of events. It happened with no warning. There was a sudden large puff of sickly green smoke, a spray of luminous green sparks, and . . . *a Genie appeared*!

As well as the smoke and the sparks, the Genie was accompanied by quite a loud thunderclap, causing several birds to fall out of trees and a passing rabbit to be treated for shock. Even Pongwiffy, who, being a Witch, was used to these things, was mildly surprised. You didn't often get

Genies in Witchway Wood. It just wasn't their sort of place. Rotten climate. Terrible food. Hardly any shops. No decent bazaars or coffee houses. No dancing girls or fire-eaters. And all those terrible old Witches.

'Bother, bother, bother!' sighed the Genie, staring around, obviously unimpressed. 'Not another wood. I have taken yet another wrong turning. How incredibly ghastly.'

'Watch it,' snapped Pongwiffy. 'This isn't just any old wood. This is Witchway Wood. I live here. So mind your tongue.'

She stared at the newcomer. He wore a filmy blouse thing under a red fringed bolero. A wide scarlet sash held up his pants. The pants were made from some flimsy material which tended to cling. On his head was a red turban. He wore far, far too much jewellery. He twinkled and clinked with trinkets, rings and bangles. Medallions hung from him like baubles on a Christmas tree. At his feet (which boasted curly-toed slippers) lay a shabby old carpet bag. He looked very out of place.

The genie's name was Ali Pali, and indeed he *was* out of place. He was also out of luck. Beneath all the flashy gear, Ali was a very worried Genie. The reason he was worried was because he was lampless. He had lost his lamp and had nowhere to go.

The reason he had no lamp to return to was simple. Somebody had dropped it. Luckily Ali was out at the time: answering a rub, building a magical palace or something. While he was gone, some nosy idiot had picked the lamp up to look at it, fumbled, then dropped it on the floor, where it smashed into a thousand pieces. Poor Ali. He had come back to find that he had lost everything, including all his nice clothes and his carefully hoarded treasure (which had been hidden up the spout). The idiot lamp-smasher had clearly pocketed that.

Every Genie lives in dread of this happening. To be without a lamp is to be mocked and sneered at by other Genies. It means you don't get invited to dinner any more. It means you have to take a *proper* job! Horrors!

Ali had to find another lamp immediately. He had to get a lid over his head without delay. The trouble was, lamps were expensive. Somehow, he would have to get enough gold together for a down payment. But how?

What was needed was some sort of cunning scam. Something which would earn him an instant fortune. Ali was rather hoping that something of this sort would present itself. On the surface, Witchway Wood didn't appear all that promising – although, funnily enough, hadn't he noticed something about it the other day in the *Genie Journal*? A small, tucked-away article about a Wall Of Smell which some enterprising old Witch had constructed in order to keep the local riff-raff from raiding her rubbish dump. Now, what was her name again?

Waving away the last of the green smoke, Ali Pali bared his teeth in his most charming smile and did one of those bows that should ideally be accompanied by the clashing of cymbals.

'A thousand pardons, madam,' he said smoothly. 'No offence intended, I am sure. Allow me to introduce myself. My name is Ali Pali. I am a Genie by profession. Ali Pali is my name, granting wishes is my game, ha ha. I am most delighted to meet you. I trust you were not startled by my sudden appearance. Please. Allow me to present you with a small gift. It is customary amongst us Genies to do this when we meet new friends.'

Still smiling his oily smile, Ali gave a theatrical snap of the fingers. There was a little puff of pink smoke, looking for all the world like airborne candyfloss, and he cleverly conjured up a gift-wrapped box full of pink Turkish delight, which floated temptingly through the air, slowly opening its own lid as it came towards Pongwiffy.

'Get it away from me!' snarled Pongwiffy, swiping bad-temperedly at the box. 'I hate Turkish delight. You Genies make me sick. You're all the same. To you it might be just another wood, but to us Witches, it's home. Clear off. You can't bribe me with your silly pink little spells. Nobody asked you to come.'

Traditionally, Witches don't trust Genies. They look down their noses at that sort of flash in the pan, showy oriental magic. They hate their towny ways and their clothes. Witches consider that Genies are slimy.

'You are right. Please. I meant no rudeness to your wood,' said Ali Pali quickly, snapping his fingers. The rejected Turkish delight vanished in an instant. 'I am just not dressed for it, you see. I am sure if I lived here I would love it. Nature. The great outdoors. The crisp smell of an autumn morning . . .'

Enthusiastically, he threw his arms wide, took a step forward and tripped over Woody. He stumbled, waving his arms wildly. One golden slipper sank into a pile of something unpleasant.

'Watch out, clumsy. That's my Broom you're treading on,' scolded Pongwiffy.

Ali Pali scraped his foot off on a clump of grass. One of his medallions had got tangled up in a nearby bramble bush, but he still managed to keep smiling.

'A thousand sorries. I sincerely apologise. But tell me. Your Broom. Why is it like this? Is it sick?'

'What's it look like?' snapped Pongwiffy.

'Hmm.' Ali Pali nudged Woody with a curly toe. 'Can I help in any way? I have a few tricks up my sleeve. I have a certain way with flying carpets. If you would allow me to examine it, perhaps I . . .'

'Look, do you mind?' said Pongwiffy, bristling crossly. This Genie was really beginning to get on her nerves. 'You're talking to a Witch, remember? I could fix it myself if I wanted to. It so happens that I don't want to, that's all.'

'Oh, fool, fool that I am!' wailed Ali Pali, striking his head in an agony of remorse. 'Of course you can fix it yourself! Why am I offering a Witch my help, poor pathetic conjuror that I am? Forgive me. If Witch Magic can't fix it, nothing can. I know that. Powerful stuff, Witch Magic. All those brews you do. All that mysterious chanting and cackling, eh? Amazing results. That Wall Of Smell, for instance. Everyone is talking about it. Even the Wizards are impressed. There's a whole article about it in the *Genie Journal*. Most interesting. Now, what was the name of the Witch who created it . . . ? It's on the tip of my tongue . . .'

Pongwiffy couldn't believe her ears. This was too good to be true.

'Me! Pongwiffy! It's me!' she burst out, unable to contain herself. 'I did it! It's my Wall. What paper was it in, did you say?'

To Pongwiffy's amazement, Ali Pali suddenly did something very unexpected. He took her hand and planted a wet, unpleasant kiss on it!

'Get off!' snapped Pongwiffy, snatching her hand back and wiping it on her sleeve. 'Yuck!'

'A thousand rejoicings!' crowed Ali Pali, hopping from one curly slipper to the other, jangling his bracelets, beside himself with pleasure. 'Fortune is with me this day! That's the name! Witch Pongwiffy! *The* Witch Pongwiffy. What an honour. Just wait till I tell the rest of the guys.'

'Well,' said Pongwiffy, terribly pleased and flattered. 'Well, fancy that. Me in the paper.'

'I am so excited!' babbled Ali Pali, wild with enthusiasm. 'The creator of the famous Wall Of Smell herself! Madam, I am your number one fan. If only I could do such Magic!'

'Oh, you probably could, in time,' said Pongwiffy graciously. She found herself warming towards this unusually charming and intelligent Genie. 'Walls Of Smell are a doddle, as a matter of fact. Kids' stuff. You only need the basic brew.'

'Please. Do not mock me. Ali Pali knows his limitations. I am but an apprentice at the craft. Pretty fireworks. Coloured lights. Pigeons. Special effects. Transformations. That's about my level. But make a *brew*? Alas. I would not know where to start. But, please. Make a humble Genie happy. I'd take it as a great honour if you'd allow me to help you carry your sick stick home.'

He bowed deeply, smiled toothily, and held out a packet of sherbet lemons.

'Sweetie?' he said.

Now, normally, Pongwiffy would have seen through all this. Warning bells would have rung and she would have rumbled his little game, no trouble. But the events of the morning had frazzled her brain. She wasn't thinking straight. Right now, she just wanted to get home. The Genie had such a nice manner. And she was particularly partial to sherbet lemons . . .

'All right,' she said, taking three. 'You take the bristle end.'

And together they set off.

'I wouldn't normally be doing this,' remarked Pongwiffy. 'We're not supposed to fraternise with you lot.'

'Quite right, best to be wary,' agreed Ali Pali. 'You can't trust anybody these days. What a charming wood this is. One moment, please. My flimsy pants are hooked up on this delightful bramble bush.'

Pongwiffy waited while he sorted himself out. There was a nasty tearing sound. They walked on in silence for a bit. Then:

'I suppose you are not allowed to talk about your great powers,' said Ali Pali. 'Such a pity. You have such an interesting personality. I could write an in-depth article for the *Journal* about you. *Pongwiffy – the Witch Behind The Smell*. That sort of thing.'

'Oh, I don't mind talking about myself,' said Pongwiffy. 'As long as you keep it general. But don't expect me to give away any trade secrets, ha ha! Any more of those sherbet lemons?'

'Certainly, certainly. Here, take the packet,' said Ali Pali. 'So you don't mind if I ask you a couple of questions, then?'

'Fire away,' said Pongwiffy amiably.

'The Wall of Smell. What's it made of?' asked Ali Pali, trying not to sound too eager.

'Aha,' said Pongwiffy. 'Old family recipe.'

'Oh, go on!' coaxed Ali Pali. 'You can trust me. As one professional to another, eh? Let me guess – would *garlic* be involved by any chance?'

'Certainly,' agreed Pongwiffy, caught off guard. 'Anti-vampire, garlic. Everyone knows that.'

'Phew!' whistled Ali Pali, lost in admiration. 'Garlic. Such brilliance!'

'The rest is just the usual,' went on Pongwiffy. 'All standard stuff. Three buckets of Eau de Stable. Four drops of Hint of Pigsty. A tablespoonful of Olde Socke. Two bad eggs. Stagnant Pond to mix. Oh, and a pinch of Skunk Powder. You mix it all up and leave to fester and ferment overnight. Then you sling it in the cauldron, bring it to the boil, stirring anti-clockwise . . .'

And so on. Ali nodded admiringly, filing it all away in his brain for future use.

'Incredible!' he said, when Pongwiffy finally

stopped talking. 'Of course, your Wall Of Smell is not exactly popular, is it? I don't agree, of course, but some say you Witches are mean old cheats. They say it wouldn't hurt to share the rubbish out a bit. Hallowe'en goodwill and so on. What do you say to that?'

Pongwiffy shrugged.

'Witches *are* mean old cheats,' she pointed out. 'That's what being a Witch is all about. If we wanted to be fair and generous we'd join the Brownies. You can quote me on that. You know what, Ali? I'm really enjoying talking to you. Any more questions?'

'Well, I've always wanted to know what makes Witch Magic so powerful.'

'That's classified information,' said Pongwiffy, 'but between you and me it's all to do with top secret Magic code numbers. Of course, only we Witches know what they are. If an enemy got hold of them, we'd be in trouble. I do know that.'

'There are many of these code numbers?'

'Oh yes. Loads. I've got them all written down in a book in my hovel.'

Such pleasant conversation helped pass the time, and finally they reached smelling distance of The Dump.

'Nearly there,' said Pongwiffy happily. 'Do you want to come in for a cup of bogwater or something? Then you can have a closer sniff of the Wall of Smell.'

'Er – no, sadly I have an appointment,' said Ali Pali, hastily dropping his end of Woody and fumbling up his sleeve for a handkerchief. 'I think we must part here. But may I say what a pleasure it's been talking to you. I do hope we meet again.'

And, with a charming little wave, he vanished.

'What a delightful Genie,' thought Pongwiffy. 'Quite the nicest I've ever come across. It just goes to show that they're not all shifty.'

Pongwiffy can sometimes be very gullible.

CHAPTER SIX
Flight

Midnight in Witchway Wood. Frost, stars and a full moon. Time for the flight! All over Witchway Wood, Witch clocks are striking twelve. All except Witch Gaga's, which strikes eighteen, gives a piercing scream, makes a muddy cup of coffee, then explodes.

At the same time, twelve Brooms stir, flex their bristles, and do a bit of sweeping just to get the sap moving. Brooms enjoy the Coven Meetings. A nice long fly followed by a good gossip. What could be nicer? A chance to have a good old moan about their owners' horrible habits, the price of a decent mop bucket and the growing threat of vacuum cleaners. Lovely.

In Pongwiffy's garden shed, Woody's limp bristles gave a twitch. It stirred, groaning. In some deep part of its being, it sensed that the hour had come and something important was about to happen.

'Thirty seconds past midnight! There you are! She's late!' Pongwiffy fretted to Hugo. 'Told you she would be. Oh, hurry up, Sharky, I'm *frozen*.'

The two of them were standing shivering in Pongwiffy's nettle patch, scanning the starry sky for their lift. Their breath steamed in the cold air. Hugo's teeth were chattering so hard he could hardly speak. October was no time to be standing nose deep in nettles at midnight. Any normal Hamster would be thinking about hibernation by now. But Hugo was no normal Hamster.

'Is c-c-cold? I not n-n-notice,' said Hugo. He even managed a casual little shrug.

That gives you an idea of how tough he was. Beneath that cute, fluffy exterior there were muscles of iron. Let other Hamsters have names like Poochy and Tiddles if they liked. That wasn't for Hugo.

Hugo had always wanted to be a Witch Familiar, and if realising his life's ambition meant freezing in a nettle patch at midnight, so be it. He just wore a scarf, blew on his paws and endured.

Pongwiffy hopped impatiently from one foot to the other. She had a battered umbrella under one arm and **How To Make Your Party Swing** under the other. Her pockets were stuffed full of pencil stubs and pieces of paper with scrawled party lists. She had throat spray, because she intended to talk a lot. If there was one thing Pongwiffy liked more than parties, it was planning parties.

'Typical, typical, typical!' she grumbled. 'She knows how much tonight means to me. She's doing it on purpose. Oh, bother that stupid Broom. It's quite spoilt my day.'

That wasn't quite true. The morning hadn't gone too well, to be sure, but Pongwiffy had quite enjoyed the rest of the day. As soon as she had arrived home, she had hurled the poor unconscious Woody into the garden shed and thrown away the key. She had then recounted the morning's dramatic events to Hugo over several cups of bogwater. She didn't mention Ali Pali. Since parting from him and his toothy smile, she had had one or two misgivings. She had a feeling she might have been rather indiscreet. She had spent the rest of the day reading *How To Make Your Party Swing* and making notes and eating bowl after bowl of reheated skunk stew. And now, at long last, it was time to go, and Sharkadder was late!

'Ze Broom is comink round, I sink,' said Hugo, hearing low clonking noises coming from the garden shed. 'Perhaps it feelink better now. Shall I go see?'

'No,' rapped Pongwiffy. 'Leave it. Stupid thing. Letting me down tonight of all nights. Sharkadder'll be here any minute. She's doing it on purpose to make me suffer. Whatever happens, Hugo, be polite to Dudley until we're airborne.'

'Look!' said Hugo suddenly, pointing a tiny paw at the sky. ''Ere zey come now.'

Sharkadder came sailing over the treetops, terribly glamorous in green. Hair, face, dress, cloak, hat, handbag, parasol, boots, everything. All green. She looked like something that had crawled from a rock pool. Slowly and sedately she descended, holding her nose. Dudley perched close behind her, looking churlish.

'Ugh!' said Sharkadder, touching down in the

nettle patch. 'That Wall Of Smell of yours is stinking up the sky, Pong. I don't know how you bear it. Well? What d'you think of the outfit? Do I look nice?'

'Incredible. You've surpassed yourself, Sharky,' lied Pongwiffy.

'I have, haven't I?' agreed Sharkadder smugly, batting her eyes and patting her verdant tangles. 'It's a miracle how I managed it considering I now have hardly any make-up to speak of. And we all know whose fault *that* is. Well, hop on, then, if you're coming. Say hello to Hugo, Dudley. If we're all going to share a Broomstick, we might as well try to be civilised.'

Dudley was sulking and wouldn't.

'Hello, fat pig cat. How ze fleas?' said Hugo sociably from Pongwiffy's shoulder. Dudley curled his lip and looked the other way, tail twitching.

'You took your time,' said Pongwiffy, jumping astride. She felt she could afford to be cocky now she was on board. 'Look, there's icicles forming on my hat we waited for so long. If you flew any slower, you'd be going backwards. I hope we're going to fly faster than that. I don't want to be late, you know.'

'Look, who's giving who a lift?' said Sharkadder

sharply. 'It's up to me how fast I fly. I'm not a sky hog like you, Pongwiffy. If there's one thing I can't stand, it's dead flies sticking to my make-up. Any more complaints, and I shan't take you. I'm still not your friend, you know. I'm only doing this under sufferance. Everybody ready for take-off? Right, Broom. Up you go!'

'Hooray!' shrieked Pongwiffy. 'Crag Hill, here we come!'

And up they went, Sharkadder's Broom labouring a bit under the extra load.

''Tis the 'amster!' hissed Dudley spitefully into Sharkadder's ear. 'The Broom can't take its weight. Shall I push it off, Mistress? Just say the word, an' I'll send it to its doom.'

'Permission to bite ze fat cat on ze bum, Mistress,' squeaked Hugo, who had heard.

'Permission denied. Stop making trouble, Hugo,' yelled Pongwiffy above the wind. 'We're guests on this Broom, remember? Look! The others! Let's catch them up!'

Sure enough, up ahead, Witches Bendyshanks, Sludgegooey, Scrofula and Ratsnappy were flying in convoy, busily swapping recipes.

'Of course, I expect I'll be asked to make my

speciality for the Hallowe'en party,' Sludgegooey was saying. 'Marshmallows. You know the secret of making marshmallows? Marsh. Plenty of it. Of course, it has to be that real, rich, black stinky stuff. Quagmire's no good, is it, Filth? Too scummy. Wrong consistency.'

The small Fiend perched on Sludgegooey's shoulder agreed that quagmire was a poor substitute for marsh.

'At a pinch, you can use swamp, but they don't come out so light – oh, hello, Sharkadder. What's Pongwiffy doing on your Broomstick?'

'I'm getting a lift,' explained Pongwiffy. 'My Broom's sick. Stick warp, we think.'

'Mine had that once,' remarked Scrofula. 'It kept shedding sawdust everywhere. What with that and my dandruff and Barry moulting, you couldn't see the floor for weeks. We were snowed in. Had to dig ourselves out with shovels in the end. Messy old business. Remember, Barry?'

The bald Vulture hunched behind her nodded sadly.

'Oh, really?' said Pongwiffy. 'Shedding sawdust, you say? It's not doing that, is it, Sharky?'

'No,' admitted Sharkadder. 'I can't say I noticed

any sawdust. Plenty of face powder, but no sawdust.'

'No sawdust, no stick warp,' said Scrofula wisely. 'It must be something else. What are the symptoms?'

'Oh – nervousness. Cold sweats. Panic attacks,' explained Pongwiffy.

'Attacks people's make-up,' chipped in Sharkadder with a bitter sniff.

'Faints a lot,' continued Pongwiffy. 'That sort of thing.'

'Sounds like it's had a shock,' remarked Bendyshanks. 'Have you tried talking to it?'

'What? In Wood, you mean? And use that language spell? No fear,' said Pongwiffy. 'I've tried kicking it, though.'

Everyone agreed that if kicking it didn't work, there was little point in talking to it.

'Have you tried being nice to it?' asked Sludgegooey. 'Stroke it. Extra rations. Treats. Kindness and sympathy can work wonders. I heard that somewhere.'

'Poppycock!' snapped Ratsnappy. 'Discipline, that's what's needed. A good, firm hand. You never see my Broom going sick. It wouldn't dare.

Sympathy is not a word in my vocabulary.'

'What word isn't in your vocabulary?' enquired a voice, and Witch Greymatter flew up alongside. She had a newspaper balanced across her stick. She was doing a crossword puzzle, and her Owl, whose name was Speks, sat on her shoulder and studied 4 Across.

'What word isn't in your vocabulary, Ratsnappy?' repeated Greymatter. 'Unquestionably it will be in mine. I flatter myself that there are very few words with which I am unfamiliar. Speks and I scour the dictionary every morning, and learn a new one. This morning we learnt VISCID. That means sludgy. Glutinous. Slimy, sticky and gluey.'

'Like your skunk stew, Pong,' said Sharkadder unkindly, and everybody except Pongwiffy nearly fell off their Broomsticks laughing.

'Very funny,' said Pongwiffy, and made a mental note to break friends with Sharkadder the minute her transportation troubles were sorted out. For ever this time.

'Here's another one,' continued Greymatter, warming to her subject. 'SAGACIOUS. It means wise. Knowledgeable. Intelligent.'

'Like you, I suppose,' growled Ratsnappy.

'Certainly. I don't want to boast, but it's obvious to everyone that I am the brains in this Coven.'

'Why?' asked everyone.

'Because I write poetry,' explained Greymatter loftily. There was no arguing with that. She did. And very highbrow it was too.

'In fact,' went on Greymatter. 'In fact, Pongwiffy, I was going to suggest that we have a poetry reading at the Hallowe'en party this year. I've written a few special verses for the occasion.'

'Er – I'm not too sure about that, Greymatter,' hedged Pongwiffy. 'I've got a few ideas of my own about the party this year.'

'Like what?' asked Ratsnappy suspiciously.

'Ah ha,' said Pongwiffy mysteriously. 'Wait and see.'

Just then, there came the sound of a horn, followed by a mad, blood-chilling screech.

'Gaga,' chorused everyone, and hastily got out of the way.

There was a fierce flapping noise, and Witch Gaga hurtled past like some demented surfer on the crest of a wave. A cloud of squeaking bats flapped adoringly around her head. She was wearing wild rags of red, white and blue, and balloons were attached to her hat. She carried a football rattle in one hand and a tin trumpet in the other. She was, of course, thoroughly bonkers – but in a jolly sort of way.

The Witches watched with interest. Gaga was celebrated for her reckless stunt work.

With a wild cry of 'Watch me, girls!' she turned two mid-air somersaults, which brought her Broom perilously close to the tip of a pine tree. Unwisely, she attempted a third, and both she and the Broom disappeared beneath the foliage, obviously destined for a spectacular crash landing.

'Seen it,' chorused the watching Witches, and flew on.

In time, more tiny figures on Broomsticks flew up to join the main convoy. The twin Witches Agglebag and Bagaggle, violins tucked beneath their chins. Witch Macabre, whose extra-long tartan-painted Broomstick had to be reinforced so that it could carry the combined weight of herself, her bagpipes and her Haggis, whose name was Rory. Grandwitch Sourmuddle and Bonidle were the last to arrive, because Sourmuddle had forgotten the time and Bonidle had overslept.

That was it. All thirteen of them. The

full ragged, chattering, squabbling complement, gliding along towards distant Crag Hill in perfect formation.

CHAPTER SEVEN
Guilt

Back in the garden shed, Woody finally came to. It sat up with a great deal of groggy groaning and head-clutching. It felt awful. It felt disorientated. Confused. It didn't know what day it was. All it knew was that it was in the shed, the shed was dark, and that it was being stared at by the Rake and the Coal Shovel, who had obviously just been talking about it behind its back.

Of course, *we* know what Woody has been through in the past twenty-four hours, and can feel some sympathy. All that talk of Goblins and axes on top of the guilty secret it was carrying. It's not surprising it cracked under the strain.

The Rake and the Shovel didn't know any of this, of course. They stared unsympathetically as Woody lurched over to its bucket and took a long, cold drink. They nudged each other as it splashed water down its stick, took deep, steadying breaths and tried to think straight. What time was it? Come to think of it, what year was it?

'Now you're in it,' said the Coal Shovel, who could never resist getting a dig in. 'Now you're in trouble. Pongwiffy's furious with you.'

'Sssh,' muttered the Rake. 'We sent it to Coventry, remember?'

'I was just saying,' explained the Shovel. 'I was just remarking that now it's in trouble. Missing the flight and that.'

Suddenly, Woody remembered everything. The Broomnapping. The Goblins. The Plan. The Meeting! Oh no! Of course, it was tonight. Even now its fellow Brooms were on their way to the Broom park. Supposing – just supposing – the Goblins actually managed to pull it off? Oh guilt, doom and alarm!

Woody gnawed its twiggy fingers, trying not

to think about what might happen to its friends. Friends that it had known since it was a sapling. Friends that it had swept with, wept with, grown with and flown with. Ashley. Little Elmer. Scotty McPine. Roots, Stumpy and all the rest. Good friends. Tried, tested and true friends. Friends who always remembered its birthday.

In an agony of remorse, Woody remembered the most important bit of the Broom Code, which said, 'A Broom sticks up for its friends.' It remembered the Broom Anthem, which went:

O riders of the sky are we!
We'll sweep away the enemy,
Till all the world exclaims, Oh, see –
There go the noble Broomsticks.

It was a moving song. It set the sap stirring, and brought tears to the eyes. Woody hummed a bit now. Strong emotion made its voice crack.

'What are you singing for?' enquired the Coal Shovel grumpily. 'You've got nothing to sing about. You're in big trouble, you. Shouldn't be surprised if it wasn't the clothes pegs this time. That'll teach you to mend yer flighty ways.'

(The Coal Shovel and Rake were always unfriendly towards Woody. They were jealous because Woody got out more than they did.)

Woody ignored them and carried on singing, louder now. It had got to the chorus, which was the best bit, the bit about Witch Broomsticks being the greatest thing since sliced bread.

'All for one and one for all,
Standing proud and straight and tall.
Sweeping, swooping, loop the looping,
Gallant, noble Broo-oom-sticks!'

'It's singing the Anthem,' observed the Rake. 'What's it doing that for?'

Woody was now singing at the top of its voice. Its eyes were glazed, its arm raised in a salute. It was changing. It was growing, straightening, standing tall and proud. It beat its stick in time to the music.

'Feeling better, are we?' sneered the Coal Shovel.

Yes. Woody *was* feeling better. Much, much better. And do you know why? Because it had made a major decision, that's why. It was the Anthem that did it. It's impossible not to come over all noble when singing such stirring words. By the time it was halfway through the chorus, it knew what it had to do. It would come clean. It would fly to the Meeting, sound the alarm, confess everything, and take the consequences. Even if it meant looking a complete twit.

Still singing, it launched into the air, smashed through the shed window and streaked away, bent on rescue.

'Show-off,' said the Coal Shovel.

'Fly boy,' agreed the Rake. And with a sniff, they both settled down to yet another everlasting game of I Spy.

'A thousand curses!'

A short way away, in Pongwiffy's hovel, Ali Pali heard the crash from the shed, snuffed out his candle and froze. It was hard to tell that it was Ali Pali, because he had swapped his turban for a balaclava. Besides, the place was in pitch darkness. However, it was indeed him. His carpet bag lay open on Pongwiffy's table. It contained various curious items. Bottles of cheap perfume. Discontinued lines of strong aftershave. Tins of air freshener. A megaphone. A cash register. Coloured flags. Crayons. A folding tent. It was amazing how it all fitted in.

After the crash came the sound of tinkling glass, followed by a sort of whoosh. After that, silence. Ali Pali waited a moment, then gave a shrug, relit his candle and continued to be up to no good.

What was he doing? He was searching for the Book of Magical code numbers. Pongwiffy *really* shouldn't have told him about that.

CHAPTER EIGHT
The Meeting

On Crag Hill, a cheery fire was blazing. Witches and Familiars milled about, chattering and gossiping and greedily eyeing the sandwiches which were piled high on trestle tables. The sandwiches were always the highlight of these affairs. The trouble was, no one was allowed to eat them until Coven business had been attended to. Which explained why the formal part of Coven Meetings always tended to be short.

The formal part hadn't yet started. Everyone was just hanging around, filling in time. Agglebag and Bagaggle practised a new duet on their violins. Ratsnappy and Scrofula picked holes in each other's knitting. Every so often, there would be a little flash of light as one of the Witches demonstrated a new spell, followed by shouts of admiration or loud ridicule, depending on how impressive it was. Further up the hill in the Broom park, the Broomsticks, parked and promptly forgotten, talked amongst themselves.

Pongwiffy was very much in evidence, talking loudly about her Broom troubles. Much to Sharkadder's disgust, she had gathered quite a crowd. All Witches consider themselves experts in such matters, and everyone had an opinion. Sharkadder was particularly annoyed when Pongwiffy acted out the bit where the Broom speared Dudley's tail and got a huge laugh. Dudley was so upset, he had to go behind a bush and bite on a rock.

'Not funny, Pongwiffy!' howled Sharkadder.

'Oh, poo! Where's your sense of humour, Sharky? Now, as I was saying . . .'

But then:

'Quiet, please!' called a shrill, imperious voice. 'If we're all ready, I'd like to call this Meeting to order. Witches, kindly be upstanding. Pass me

251

my umbrella, Snoop. If they don't stop yapping, Macabre, give 'em a blast on your bagpipes.'

The voice belonged to Grandwitch Sourmuddle, Mistress of the Witchway Coven. Over two hundred years old, with a shocking memory. Firelight glinted on her spectacles, and on the pitchfork of the small, exasperated Demon who perched on her shoulder, forked tail draped around her neck like a long scarf. His name was Snoop, and he was Sourmuddle's Familiar.

Witch Macabre threateningly raised her pipes to her lips. Rory, her Haggis, gave a warning moo. Immediately, the gossip and chatter died down. Knitting was put away, noses blown and coughs stifled. Witches and Familiars stood to attention. Those who had remembered umbrellas opened them. The rest stood with hunched shoulders, looking resigned.

'Hail, Witches!' piped the Grandwitch.

'Hail!' came the response. As always, a small cloud came buzzing through the sky and delivered a short, sharp burst of hailstones before busily whizzing off again.

'I declare the formal bit of this Meeting open,' announced Sourmuddle, folding her umbrella.

'Right. Park yer bums.'

There was an immediate scramble for a warm spot in front of the fire. After a great deal of jostling and pushing, they were all finally sitting comfortably. (Or in Gaga's case, hanging comfortably from a nearby tree.) Pongwiffy made sure she was in the middle of the front row. Hugo climbed on to the rim of her hat, where he could see better. On one side of them sat Sharkadder and Dudley. On the other slumped Witch Bonidle and her Sloth, who was acting as a pillow. As usual, they were both fast asleep. A half-eaten apple dangled from Bonidle's limp hand. Pongwiffy pinched it and finished it off for her. That's Witch behaviour for you.

Scrofula stuck her hand in the air.

'Excuse me, Sourmuddle. Can Barry and I be excused? Neither of us are feeling too well. If you don't mind, we'd like to take our share of the sandwiches and go home. I've got a sore throat, and Barry's moulting again, aren't you, Barry?'

She nudged the sad, bald vulture, and he gave an obliging cough.

'Not likely,' said Sourmuddle. 'You're going to stay here and suffer with the rest of us. Yes,

Sharkadder? What's the matter with you?'

'Grandwitch Sourmuddle, I've got a complaint about Pongwiffy. Do you know what she did? Or rather, what she let her Broom do. She . . .'

'Later, Sharkadder, later. You know that complaints about Pongwiffy come under Any Other Business. First things first. We are here tonight to discuss . . . er . . . we are here to . . . what are we here to discuss, Snoop?'

There was a general sigh.

'The Hallowe'en Party,' Snoop reminded her wearily. 'I've told you a thousand times.'

'Yes, yes, I knew all the time, I was just testing you. Find the Coven Account Book, will you? And somebody wake up Bonidle. I can't hear myself think with her snoring like that.'

Snoop raised his eyes to heaven, slid down and rummaged about in a black plastic bin liner. It was full of all kinds of junk. Spell books, Wands, magical potions, crystal balls and the odd toad or two were all jumbled up with a flask of hot soup, gumboots, cough medicine, corn plasters and an extra scarf for the flight home. Sourmuddle liked to be prepared. Finally, a dog-eared old exercise book came to light.

Meanwhile, Pongwiffy helpfully tried to wake Bonidle, who, you will remember, was fast asleep, head on Sloth. (The Sloth, incidentally, doesn't have a name. Bonidle is too lazy to think of one, and the Sloth is too tired to care.)

Pongwiffy's method of awakening the sleeping beauty was to administer a sharp dig in the ribs with the handle of her umbrella. Accidentally on purpose, she managed to poke Sharkadder up the nose with the sharp end. For Sharkadder, this was the final straw. The uneasy truce between them was broken.

'Idiot!' hissed Sharkadder. 'That's it! As of now, I am no longer your friend! You can walk home.'

'If I walk home, you don't get to judge the Fancy Dress,' threatened Pongwiffy. 'And you can't be in it either,' she added.

'Be quiet, Pongwiffy and Sharkadder,' scolded Grandwitch Sourmuddle. 'This is an important Meeting. It's essential that we pay attention. We have to discuss the Hallowe'en party.'

'Is that all?' complained Witch Macabre. 'Can we noo have a friendly wee fisticuffs, then? Ah'm really in the mood.'

'Sorry to disappoint you, Macabre, but there's no

fighting tonight.'

Macabre went into a sulk, and Rory pawed the ground with a frustrated hoof. (Rory is interesting. Macabre insists that he is the only live Haggis in existence. Looking at him, that is probably just as well. He has a great deal of shaggy fur and a daft-looking fringe which hangs over his eyes.)

'Pongwiffy?' called Sourmuddle. 'I've got a horrible feeling it's your turn to organise the party this year.'

'It certainly is, Sourmuddle!' yelled Pongwiffy, leaping to her feet, sticking her arm in the air, quivering with keenness. 'This year's party will be the best yet!'

'Wrong,' said Sourmuddle, opening the Account Book. 'Terrible news, I'm afraid. We can't afford a party this year. We're out of funds.'

This announcement was greeted with loud moans. Pongwiffy couldn't believe her ears.

'*No party?*' she shrieked. 'But it's my *turn*, Sourmuddle. Of course we must have a party. I've got loads of wonderful ideas!'

'Well, all right, perhaps no party at all is going a bit far,' relented Sourmuddle. 'But we'll have to cut out a few things. Like the balloons, the funny hats, the barbecue, the band, the prizes, the cake, the party bags, the . . .'

'Stop, stop! You're cutting everything out. There's nothing left!' wailed Pongwiffy.

'Yes, there is. We can bring sandwiches, like we did tonight. And we can still sit and cackle around the bonfire. I'm sorry, Pongwiffy. I know you think you're the world's best organiser, though I can't think why. But if we haven't got any money, there's not a lot we can do, is there? Right. Meeting over. Let's eat.'

The consensus seemed to be that this was a jolly good idea. There was a general stirring and rising and scrabbling about for Wands and handbags. Until . . .

'Hold it right there!' Pongwiffy wasn't about to give in that easily. 'Certainly we must have a proper party! Where's our pride? Do we not have a reputation to uphold? Are we not the best party givers this side of the Misty Mountains? Of course we are. Sandwiches! Cackling around bonfires! Ha!'

'What's wrong with cackling around bonfires?' demanded Ratsnappy. 'We've always cackled around bonfires on Hallowe'en. It's tradition.'

'Aye!' agreed Macabre. 'We've heard your

crackpot ideas befoor, Pongwiffy. Ah'm all foor tradition.'

'Nonsense,' said Pongwiffy. 'Don't be such old stick-in-the-muds. I've got a brilliant idea for this year's party which'll really put this Coven on the map. It comes from this wonderful book which I found and just happen to have right here.'

With a bold gesture, she held the crumbling edition of *How To Make Your Party Swing* above her head.

'Listen!' she shrieked with the glassy-eyed conviction of the converted. 'What about *this* for an idea, then? A Fancy Dress parade!'

A long silence. Apart from Sharkadder, blank faces. Nobody had ever heard of such a thing before. The trouble was, nobody wanted to be the first to admit it.

'Not that it matters, as we can't afford it anyway – but what's Fancy Dress?' asked Sourmuddle, who was too old to care about seeming silly. Everyone breathed a sigh of relief.

'Ah! Well, we dress up as someone or something else, you see,' explained Pongwiffy. 'It can be anything. And there'll be a prize for the best costume.'

258

'I knew that,' Sharkadder told everyone knowledgeably. 'It's a very modern idea, actually.'

'When you say it can be *anything*, what exactly do you mean?' enquired Greymatter. 'You mean, a queen or a penguin or a bar of soap?'

'Exactly right, Greymatter,' beamed Pongwiffy. 'You've got the idea. We could dress up as Stone Age cavewomen if we liked. In sabre-toothed tiger skins.'

'A bit chilly,' pointed out Sourmuddle. 'Crag Hill's not the warmest of spots in October. I've got three vests on now, and an extra cardi. Besides, where am I supposed to lay my hands on a sabre-toothed tiger skin? They're extinct, aren't they?'

Pongwiffy sighed. This was going to be an uphill struggle.

'No, no, Sourmuddle. I just said cavewomen as an *example*. You might want to be something completely different. Robin Hood. A pencil. A princess. Anything you like. You choose. See?'

There was another long silence, while everybody thought about it. Fancy Dress, eh? Wearing something other than rags for a change. Hmm. It took a bit of getting used to. On the other hand, it

259

might be a bit of fun. Especially if there was a prize.

'That's all very well, Pongwiffy,' said Bendyshanks, 'but we can't even afford to buy a cake. Where do we get the money for costumes, may I ask?'

'I'll get it!' promised Pongwiffy rashly. 'I'll get the money, don't you worry. I've got the rubbish for the bonfire, I might as well do everything else. Don't worry, girls, not only will we have a party this year, but it'll be the best one yet! Just wait till you hear the rest of my ideas. What I propose is this . . .'

But she got no further. Instead, there came an interruption. There was a whistling noise from high above, and something long and thin came hurtling out of the sky, straight as an arrow, whizz, bang, down into their midst.

CHAPTER NINE
Communication Problems

Who was this unexpected visitor? Woody, of course. Bold, determined Woody, all set to avert disaster by heroically coming clean.

'Oh no,' muttered Pongwiffy to Hugo. 'It's going to show me up again. I just know it.'

'It's that wretched Broom again!' cried Sharkadder. 'I thought you said you locked it in the shed, Pongwiffy. What's it doing here? Look, everyone, Pongwiffy's Broom! It's flown here all on its own, and that's against the rules, isn't it, Sourmuddle? That deserves three black marks at least.'

'Objection!' protested Pongwiffy. 'It's not *my* fault it's here, is it? Home! Home this minute, Broom.'

This brought a storm of protest. Nobody wanted to lose the Broom just yet. All Witches love talking about illnesses, especially operations. They consider themselves experts at diagnosing faults in their equipment, whether it be Wands, cauldrons or Broomsticks. Everyone had a pet theory about Pongwiffy's ailing Broom. Suggestions ranged from high sap pressure to Acute Nerves Brought On By Living With Pongwiffy. They were all terribly keen to observe the patient in the flesh – or wood, rather.

Besides, Pongwiffy's Broom was really most entertaining. Amongst other things, it was licking Pongwiffy's boots, would you believe!

'Sharkadder's quite right, Pongwiffy,' said Sourmuddle. 'That Broom shouldn't be out on its own. No Flying Without A Witch. It says so clearly in the Rule Book.'

'But, Sourmuddle, I left it in the shed!' protested Pongwiffy. 'It's not my fault if it followed me. Oh, do stop it, Broom! Down! You're behaving like an idiot!'

She was right. Woody was. It had finished

boot-licking, and was now jumping about like a badly trained puppy. It was making short, agitated little runs, pointing urgently up the hill, beckoning, then coming back to tug at her cardigan sleeve. Pongwiffy was terribly embarrassed, and smacked it hard on the stick.

'It wants to go walkies,' remarked Bendyshanks with a smirk. 'Look! It thinks it's a dog!'

'Give it a bone, Pongwiffy!' jeered Sludgegooey to general laughter.

'Woof woof!' barked Agglebag and Bagaggle, rocking with the giggles.

'No control,' sneered Ratsnappy. 'Firm handling, that's what Brooms need.'

'Excuse me, Grandvitch Sourmuddle,' said Hugo. 'I sink zis Broom is tryink to tell us sumsink. It got big, important news for us, zis Broom. I sure of it.'

'Well, we can find out soon enough,' said Sourmuddle. 'Use that language spell, Pongwiffy, and ask it. You know. *Zithery zithery zoom . . .*'

'Never,' said Pongwiffy firmly. 'Ever tried using that spell, Sourmuddle?'

'Well, yes, I see what you mean,' admitted Sourmuddle. 'Awful side effects. Any volunteers to speak Wood? In the cause of medical science?'

There were none, of course. Even in the cause of medical science, none of the Witches could face those awful side effects. One or two lost interest altogether, and began to drift towards the sandwiches.

Poor Woody. What an anticlimax. It had come all this way, perfectly prepared to do the honourable thing and take the consequences. But it had forgotten one critical thing. Nobody could speak Wood.

'Can it write?' enquired Scrofula, not very hopefully.

'Only in Wood,' said Pongwiffy. So that was no good.

'I have a suggestion. It could tap out a message in Morse code!'

That was Witch Greymatter. At the time, it seemed like a good idea.

'Broom!' ordered Pongwiffy sternly. 'Kindly take yourself over to that tree and tap out whatever you have to say in Morse code.'

At last! They were making some headway! Everyone crowded round and listened hard while Woody carefully tapped out the message on a tree trunk. DANGER. BE PREPARED.

GOBLINS PLANNING TO RAID BROOM
PARK TONIGHT. FORGOT TO MENTION
EARLIER. SORRY. MY FAULT. YOURS
SINCERELY, WOODY.

Sadly, when it finally reached the end, it turned
out that no one could understand Morse code
anyway. It was all most terribly frustrating.

'I know! It can act it out!' suggested Sludgegooey.
'You know, like in charades. One word at a time.'

'What d'you think, Broom?' asked Pongwiffy.
'Think you can do it?'

Woody thought it unlikely. It had never thought
of itself as an actor. But desperate measures were
called for. It held up one twiggy finger.

'First word,' chorused everyone, clustering
round. This was more like it. This was fun. This was
entertainment. Next to eating, casting spells and
talking about illnesses, if there's one thing Witches
enjoy, it's charades.

Woody hesitated for a moment. Then it made
a sudden sideways lunge at Witch Scrofula, who
happened to be wearing a woolly red scarf. Scrofula
gave a squawk of protest as her favourite neck
warmer was snatched away and waved furiously in
the air.

'Scarf,' said Greymatter. 'It's trying to tell us it's got a sore throat. That's obvious.'

Wild with frustration, Woody shook its head and flapped the scarf some more.

'It wants to do some knitting,' suggested Sharkadder. 'It's bored and feels like a bit of a knit. Looks like one too,' she added unkindly.

'Leave it alone, Sharkadder,' said Pongwiffy. 'It's doing its best.'

'I know vat it tryink to show,' said Hugo, who was very good at charades. 'It try to show ze colour red. Red for danger. Right, Broom?'

Woody nodded emotionally. It could have wept with gratitude. Now they were getting somewhere. Everyone cheered, and Hugo took a bow. Scrofula snatched back her scarf, and sullenly wound it round her neck.

'Ze first vord is *danger*. Zis ve know. Vat next?'

Woody thought for a moment. This next one was going to stretch its talent to the utmost limits. First, it cupped its ear.

'*Sounds like*,' chorused one and all, caught up in the spirit of the thing. Encouraged, Woody suddenly winced, as though its bristles hurt. It then began to walk very slowly, swaying from side to side.

We know what it was doing, don't we? Hobbling. Because hobbling sounds vaguely like Goblin, and that was all it could think of.

'It's limping!' yelled Filth, Sludegooey's Fiend. 'What sounds like limp?'

'Chimp! There's a wild chimp on the loose?' guessed Witch Ratsnappy, suddenly inspired. But Woody was shaking its head. That wasn't it. They all thought again.

'Shuffling?'

'Blisters?'

'Athlete's foot? Bad leg?'

The suggestions kept coming, all wrong, wrong, hopelessly wrong. Woody was getting near the end of its tether. Its fevered imagination conjured up the sound of far crashings and muffled cries coming from the direction of the Broom park, which was clearly under attack *right now*. It simply *had* to make these idiot Witches understand. Desperately, it thought of its own personal motto – 'Stick with it' – and tried hobbling harder . . .

CHAPTER TEN
The Raid

So. What *was* happening in the Broom park?
Not a lot.

The Brooms were propped against various trees, engaged in deep discussion. They always enjoyed their monthly get-togethers, but tonight was even better because, for once, they had something interesting to talk about. Real, hot news! Almost bordering on scandal, really. Heard about old Woody? No. What? Some sort of breakdown. Really? Oooooh. Yep. Too ill to fly. You don't say! Poor old stick. Chucked in the garden shed, did you say? Tut tut. What a shame.

Eagerly, they compared notes. Unlike Witches, Brooms are a tender-hearted bunch when one of their friends feels a bit below par. There was a great deal of sympathetic tutting. Sharkadder's Broom, Ashley (Woody's best friend), shed a tear or two and proposed buying a Get Well card which they would all sign. There was talk of having a collection and sending along a bunch of flowers. Sourmuddle's Broom, Stumpy, went one better, and daringly proposed that they should pay Woody a flying visit. Now. While the Witches were busy. They were sure to be hours yet. If the Brooms left right now, there would just be time to whizz along to Woody's shed and cheer up their mate. Maybe stop off somewhere and buy a few grapes. Surprise, surprise! Bet you didn't expect us, etc. All right, so it wasn't strictly allowed, but in the circumstances, surely ... ? Besides, Woody's illness sounded quite spectacular. Though they wouldn't admit it, they were all keen to have a good old gawp.

Crack! What was that?

The snap of a twig, a muffled sneeze. Oh dear. Who's that creeping up under cover of the bushes? They were so concerned and caring, those Brooms,

269

so caught up in their friend's sorry plight that they didn't notice they were being sneaked up on by . . .

Goblins! Yes. It's them all right. Incredible as it might seem, Plugugly, Slopbucket, Lardo, Hog, Sproggit, Stinkwart and Eyesore have actually made it! They have walked on tiptoe all the way from Goblin Territory to Crag Hill. It has taken them hours and hours, but they are here. As far as they are concerned, they are about to carry out the biggest Broomnapping in the whole of history.

The Goblins are really trying hard with this one, and to give credit where it's due, they haven't done too badly at all so far. A few minor details have gone wrong, but they've got the most important things right. For a start, they have remembered to come. They also have the correct evening. They have even made an effort to disguise themselves. Plugugly is wearing a false nose, Lardo and Hog have done things with paper bags, and the others are got up as bushes.

They are doing other things right too. They are attempting to blend into the shadows. They are downwind of their prey. They have a secret password, which none of them can pronounce. The word is UNPRONOUNCEABLE.

In the dark, it's difficult to tell friend from foe, so they keep whispering it, just to be on the safe side. In between attempting to pronounce unpronounceable, they are making the sort of noises that they feel small woodland creatures might make, in case the Brooms get suspicious. They are armed to the teeth with everything you might possibly need for a mass Broomnapping. Sacks, ropes, nets, gags, pitchforks, string, and a large bag of stolen humbugs. Ten out of ten for effort.

It was a terribly tense time for the Goblins. They never, ever managed to do anything right, and they all felt the strain. It would be so nice if, just once, a Goblin Plan worked properly – but it was always the same. Whatever they attempted – be it a simple hunting trip, a raid on Pongwiffy's rubbish dump, or tying up their bootlaces – they always seemed to mess it up. Plugugly was particularly nervous, because it was his very own Plan.

It went like this.

1. Creep up in disguise
2. Capture Brooms
3. Take Brooms Home in Cart
5. Hide Brooms!

271

This was very detailed for a Goblin Plan and Plugugly was rightfully proud of it. He normally just fell in with other people's plans, but this one he had thought up all by himself. That made him the leader. So he was responsible for attending to the details. For checking the equipment. For telling everyone what to do. For making sure they did it. No wonder he was nervous.

It was good, though, being the leader. Plugugly was enjoying the novelty of it all. When he realised that he could boss people around, he told Sproggit to oil the wheels of the stolen cart. The one they would use to carry the Broomnapping equipment to Crag Hill and the victims back to Goblin Territory.

That was the first thing that went wrong. Sproggit forgot. So the cart had squeaked most irritatingly as the Goblins tiptoed all the way from Goblin Territory to Crag Hill – and believe me, that's a very long way. A squeaking cart rather tends to spoil the element of surprise. So they had abandoned it and carried the equipment the rest of the way.

The disguises hadn't really worked that well. Everyone and everything they met along the way recognised them instantly and fell about laughing. That was disappointing. However, Plug ugly consoled himself with the thought that they hadn't yet mucked up anything major. Part 1 of the Plan – Creeping Up In Disguise – was now complete. Time for Part 2, which was Capture Brooms. The Goblins had rehearsed this bit over and over again. At the signal – which was Plugugly shouting, 'Ready, Steady, Go!' – they would all leap out with nets and ropes and so on, grab the Brooms, wrestle them to the ground, and bind and gag them.

This bit of the Plan was hopeless. It had more holes in than the nets the Goblins had brought. They never got it right in rehearsals, when there weren't even any real Brooms. For a start, Plugugly never managed to say 'Ready, Steady, Go!' in the right order, so the Goblins never managed to leap at the same time. Somebody always tripped over. Nobody was quite sure what to do once he'd wrestled his Broom to the ground. Supposing it wrestled back? Brooms were as slippery as eels, if Pongwiffy's was anything to go by. There they were, then, hiding behind trees and bushes, waiting for the signal, feeling horribly nervous. Plugugly adjusted his false nose, licked his lips, and tried to remember the order of the words. How did it go again?

'Reddysteddygo,' muttered Plugugly to himself.

'Reddysteddygo. Dat's it. Right den. 'Ere goes. Er . . . REDDYGOSTEDDY!'

Poor Plugugly. The most important thing he'd ever had to do, and he mucked it up. The rest of the Goblins stared at each other, wondering whether they should leap now or make Plugugly do it again and get it right. Sproggit, Slopbucket and Lardo hesitantly leapt. Hog, Eyesore and Stinkwort remained where they were. Sproggit, Slopbucket and Lardo ran back again, red with embarrassment. It was a farce. But it didn't matter either way. Because at exactly the moment that Plugugly mucked it up, the Brooms suddenly took off! Just like that, of their own accord. No warning, straight up, all together. Once airborne, they hovered for a moment – then, as one, they turned and flew off in a southerly direction. They were off to visit their ol' mate Woody. They didn't even know that they'd been sneaked up on, let alone leapt out at.

The Goblins watched, open-mouthed, as the Brooms flew away. There was a long silence. Then . . .

'Typical,' remarked young Sproggit with a shrug. Which it was.

CHAPTER ELEVEN
A state of emergency

Meanwhile, back down the hill, the game of charades continued. Woody's performance was going from strength to strength. Before or since, no Broom has ever hobbled quite as convincingly and sincerely as Woody hobbled that night. It had found a stick, and was using it as a crutch. It winced at every step. Desperation lent real strength and majesty to its performance. So it wasn't surprising that, at long last, Hugo got it!

''Obbling!' squeaked Hugo. 'Ze Broom is 'obbling!'

Woody almost wept with relief.

'Oh, well done, Hugo,' said Pongwiffy, patting him on the back. 'Now then. What sounds like hobbling? Bobbling, cobbling – hey! Gobbling, of course! And gobbling sounds like Goblin. I knew it! Remember, Sharky? It came over all weird earlier when we mentioned Goblins. I'm right, aren't I, Broom?'

Drained by its performance, Woody gave a weak nod, and there was general relief all round. Everyone was having a great time. Well, not quite everyone. Sharkadder was annoyed because Pongwiffy was the centre of attention yet again. Dudley was vexed because Hugo had been the shining star of this particular game of charades. Macabre and Rory were missing. Bonidle was asleep, and a few of the Familiars had lost interest and were talking amongst themselves. But apart from *that*, everybody was having a great time.

'Right,' Pongwiffy summed up, 'we have Danger, Goblins. Now we have to get the next bit. You've done all right so far, Broom. We've seen some brilliant acting tonight, eh, girls?'

Scattered applause. Woody gave a weak bow.

'Concentrate, Broom,' urged Hugo. 'Ve need to

know *vere* and *vat* is zis danger of vich you speak. Please act out ze next vord.'

But Woody never got the chance. A sound of galloping hooves came from the trees and Macabre, mounted on Rory, crashed into the glade. Her hat was over one eye, and she was bursting with importance. She was shouting and whooping and waving something triumphantly on high.

It was a grubby Goblin bobble hat!

Macabre pulled on the reins sharply, and Rory skidded to a halt.

'Treachery!' howled Macabre. 'Treachery and skulduggery! The Brooms ha' bin nicked, every last one. We bin robbed, girrls. And d'ye ken who by? Goblins, that's who. Look! Look what Ah foond!'

Macabre speared the evidence on the end of her bagpipes and waved it under people's noses.

Alarm and consternation! Cries of anger, flapping of wings, flexing of claws, gnashing of teeth, shaking of fists. Panic, accusations, and a lot of running around and shouting. Two cases of hysterics, and three of fainting. Macabre wanted to form a posse. Greymatter wanted to take a vote. Gaga fell out of her tree. Agglebag and Bagaggle came over all funny and took turns fanning each

278

other. It wasn't often that such dramatic events occurred during Coven Meetings, and the Witches wanted to get their money's worth. In the midst of it all, Pongwiffy was leaping up and down in a ripe royal fury, giving Woody a piece of her mind.

'Idiot! Nincompoop! Stupid, dozy, wooden-brained plank-head! I see it all now. You got caught by Goblins, didn't you? That's where you were all that time when you went missing. You overheard their plans, didn't you? You knew all along about this, you great sap. You useless cleaning utensil. Why didn't you tell me before? Twig brain!'

Woody hung its head and said nothing. From great actor to useless cleaning utensil in ten easy insults. Oh, the shame of it all. It was now a broken Broom who deserved everything that Pongwiffy threw at it.

'All right, all right, that's enough. No need to get carried away. Calm down, everyone!' ordered Grandwitch Sourmuddle severely. 'What's all the fuss? It's only Goblins. And Goblins are bungling idiots, remember? They don't even have Magic. Watch me. I'll get our Brooms back with a flick of my Wand. Where's my Wand, Snoop?'

'In your hand,' pointed out Snoop.

'Just testing. Right, then. Watch the sky for returning Broomsticks. *Head of beer and tail of deer, make our Broomsticks reappear!*

And Sourmuddle gave her Wand a little flick. Now, at this point, something impressive should have happened. A rumble of thunder, maybe, and a flash of lightning. At the very least, green smoke. The night sky should then have swarmed with prodigal Broomsticks. A glad reunion should have followed. The Goblins would have been captured and dealt with most severely. Then everyone could have eaten the sandwiches and gone home.

Not so this time. Everyone was eagerly craning upwards, but nothing happened. Well, that's not quite right. What happened was that Sourmuddle's Wand gave a feeble little *phut,* sprayed a few green sparks, then went limp.

'That's worrying,' said Grandwitch Sourmuddle, flopping it about like a length of liquorice. 'Only had it serviced recently. Hmm. I wonder. Everyone had better inspect their equipment.'

Alarmed Witches scrabbled in their pockets and handbags. It's surprising how much a Witch can get in her handbag. Wands, bells, books, candles, crystal balls, even fold-up cauldrons were produced, along with a load of dirty hankies, small frogs, tooth-less combs, photographs of loved ones and fluffy old half-sucked boiled sweets. There was a lot of flicking and muttering and peering and little exclamations of dismay.

'Sourmuddle! My Wand's gone wonky too!' shouted Pongwiffy importantly. 'Look, it's all floppy, see? Just like yours.' Nobody took any notice. Pongwiffy's equipment seldom worked, mainly because she never cleaned it.

'I don't know about you lot, but my crystal ball's up the creek,' said Sourmuddle. 'Might as well try to see into a cowpat.'

Crystal ball owners excitedly agreed that theirs were displaying the same mysterious symptoms.

'And guess what! The pages of my Pocket Spell Book are all stuck up with mysterious invisible glue,' cried Sludgegooey. 'It's usually egg,' she explained to anyone who was interested.

'Oh no! My best wishbone's snapped!'

'Look, everybody, I can't make little green explosions any more! See? I snapped my fingers and nothing happened.'

'I don't know about you lot, but my brain's gone blank. I can't even remember the ingredients for a basic brew!'

It was true. Bells wouldn't ring, books wouldn't open and candles wouldn't light. Brains refused to come up with the simplest spell. There wasn't a stiff Wand to be seen. Wand droop was the order of the day.

'Sabotage!' hissed Sourmuddle thrillingly. 'Sabotage, shenanigans and hanky panky. You know what, Witches? There's another Power at work, blocking ours. I've come across this sort of thing before. Some cheeky upstart has got hold of our top secret Magic code numbers. The ones we're never supposed to reveal on pain of being lowered into a well and pelted with bad eggs. All right, you lot, who's been giving out inside information? Come on, come on, it's obvious that one of you has been shooting her mouth off.'

That was when Pongwiffy had a rather nasty coughing fit. It was so bad, she had to go behind a tree for a moment.

'Oh well, there's only one thing to do,' continued Sourmuddle. 'I hereby declare an Official State Of Emergency.'

There was a loud cheer. Official State of Emergency, eh? They didn't have one of those very often. It sounded terribly exciting.

'Basically, girls, we're in a bit of a fix. No Magic. No transport. It's obvious somebody's up to no good behind our backs! But who?'

'Booo! Just wait till we get our hands on 'em!'

'Grrr!'

There was a lot of enthusiastic shouting. Pongwiffy got over her coughing fit, stepped casually out from her tree, and shouted louder than anyone.

'Why did you go behind that tree just then, Pongwiffy?' asked Sharkadder, sidling up.

'Mind your own business,' said Pongwiffy. 'Grrr! Boo! Down with cheeky upstarts!'

'Who? Who?' pondered Sourmuddle. 'Who's got the nerve to mess with Witches on the run-up to Hallowe'en?'

Everyone thought hard. It wasn't likely to be the Wizards, who were far too snooty. Likewise the Skeletons. The Ghouls didn't have the nerve. The Goblins didn't have the brains, did they? Although there was the bobble hat, of course . . .

'I'm fed up wi' all this talk,' announced Macabre, who was a Witch of action. 'I'm goin' back tay the Broom park tay look for more clues.' And she mounted on Rory and rode off.

'Oh well, there's nothing else for it,' decided Sourmuddle. 'Where are you, Pongwiffy?'

'Me? Why? What d'you want me for?' demanded Pongwiffy, terribly flustered to be picked on.

'You'll just have to fly off and find out what's going on,' explained Sourmuddle. 'You're the only one with transport, remember? So it's up to you to sort it out. Besides, if you had proper control over your Broom none of this would have happened. So I hold you personally responsible for getting our Brooms back. Off you go. And don't take all night about it.'

'What – all on my own?' complained Pongwiffy, glancing hopefully at Sharkadder. Sharkadder tossed her hair, linked her arm in Sludgegooey's and purposely turned her back.

'Don't be such a baby, Pongwiffy,' said Sourmuddle, impatient to get at the sandwiches. 'Off you go. One Witch is more than a match for Goblins. Even you.'

'But my Wand's not working and my Broom might not be well enough to fly and I don't even know where to start looking and we haven't finished discussing the party . . .'

'Stop making excuses,' said Sourmuddle. 'We're in a State of Emergency. It's hardly the time to think about parties, is it? Hardly the time to think about enjoying ourselves. Hey, Agglebag! Grab me one of those spiderspread sandwiches, will you? Now, buzz off, Pongwiffy, and don't come back without those Broomsticks.'

And in seconds, the trestle tables were under attack and Pongwiffy, Hugo and the disgraced Woody were left quite alone. Nobody offered to accompany them on their mission. Sharkadder was tucking in without even glancing in Pongwiffy's direction.

Oh well. There was nothing else for it. Grimly, Pongwiffy grabbed Woody. It shied nervously, then held steady as Pongwiffy clambered aboard.

'Vere ve go first, Mistress?' asked Hugo, scuttling up to the rim of her hat.

'Up,' said Pongwiffy irritably. 'Where else?'

Desperate to please, Woody went up.

CHAPTER TWELVE
Cleaning Up

How Ali Pali ever managed to organise such a major event in the time will always remain a mystery. You have to hand it to him. When it came to transformations, that Genie was a genius.

The Dump had been taken over and changed beyond all recognition. It now looked like a sort of cross between a rubbish dump and an oriental fairground. It had an exotic, Aladdinish sort of allure. It was brilliantly illuminated. Coloured magic lanterns. Fairy lights. Bunting. Flags. That sort of thing.

Ali Pali obviously believed in heavy advertising. There were posters tacked up on trees all over Witchway Wood, advertising the event in huge, screaming letters.

TONIGHT! GRAND RAID ON RUBBISH DUMP! EVERYTHING MUST GO! FIVE QUID ONLY FOR TEN MINUTES' UNINTERRUPTED LOOTING! BRING YOUR FRIENDS! HAVE FUN! WALL OF SMELL DISMANTLED COURTESY OF GENIE ENTERPRISES.

Yes, indeed, the Wall of Smell had gone. The Dump now smelt strongly of the antidote (the main ingredient of which was a cheap eastern hair oil called Desert Pong).

At the entrance, a striped tent had been erected. Inside, Ali Pali sat cross-legged on a pile of cushions, stuffing fivers into a till. He was equipped with a megaphone and a very fancy pocket watch which he consulted regularly. His carpet bag lay at his feet. A large ruby was flashing on one of the medallions around his neck, otherwise you would never have known that he was simultaneously working very complicated Magic. Erecting a barrier on all incoming spells from Crag Hill to be precise.

It's all rather technical and hard to understand unless you're a paid-up member of the Magic Circle.

A long queue stretched far back into the Wood. It consisted of the usual crowd. A languid group of Skeletons; a gang of Ghouls, behaving like louts as always; the local chapter of the Hell's Gnomes; a bevy of Banshees and a troupe of Trolls; several hairy types you couldn't really put a name to. Everyone clutched handbills saying *All You Can Carry For A Fiver* and wore expressions of barely contained glee. They had been itching to get their hands on Pongwiffy's rubbish for weeks.

Two buskers entertained the waiting hordes. A tap-dancing Gnome with a banjo attempted to drown out a Leprechaun who sang a sad song about his grey-haired ol' mudder. Every so often they would stop to pass their hats around.

Once inside, the fun really started. There was better class entertainment for a start. A tall, quiet chap with a bolt through his neck played the spoons. An enterprising Fiend was selling commemorative badges saying 'I Raided Pong's Dump' followed by the date. A lipsticky Gnome in big earrings had taken over Pongwiffy's garden shed and turned it into a fortune-telling booth where she dished out lashings of doom to anyone fool enough to poke his nose in. In order to give herself room she had turfed out a rusty old rake and an ancient coal shovel she'd found cluttering up the place.

There were refreshments too. As the ultimate insult, Pongwiffy's hovel had been turned into a tea hut. Her very own kitchen table and chairs had been placed outside, and two Yetis in grubby aprons moved around with a tray, wiping up spills with *one of Pongwiffy's very own cardigans!*

Next to the tea hut, there was the inevitable hot frogs stall. The hot frogs were proving rather more popular than the vegetarian alternatives – a choice of fungus burgers or curried nettles served on a bed of lightly toasted pine needles.

But the main attraction, of course, was The Rubbish. Perfect bonfire fodder. It made you drool. It made you want to dance and sing. It made you go a bit funny in the head. All that lovely rubbish, just sitting there waiting to be stolen. Yipppeeeee!

Once the punters were inside, a sort of rubbish fever came over them. They raced madly for the teetering piles, falling on choice items with wild triumphant cries. Some dived head first and vanished. The lucky ones got rescued by their

289

mates. It was like gold prospectors coming across a particularly rich seam.

Everyone seemed to have their favourite sort of junk. The Skeletons, efficient as ever, formed a non-human chain and passed prized ultra-burnable chair legs along the line into the boot of a waiting hearse. Two Mummies bumbled around with a horsehair sofa. They kept bumping into things as they tried to find the exit.

The local chapter of Hell's Gnomes jealously guarded a pile of old motorbike tyres. The Ghouls seemed to go in for old newspapers in a big way and were carting off hundreds of mouldy back issues of *Witch Weekly* and *The Daily Miracle*. Two Werewolves, having the double advantages of superhuman strength and nasty sets of gnashers, got more than their fair share of the ever-popular broken wardrobes. A small Dragon by the name of Arthur made off triumphantly with a whole grand piano, giggling to himself.

A demented-looking furry Thing with a T-shirt which said *Moonmad* hurtled around with an old pram. It was clearly an indecisive sort of Thing, as it kept changing its mind, emptying everything out, and starting all over again. The abandoned junk was then swooped on and picked over by Banshees with shopping bags and a Troll with a stolen supermarket trolley.

It was a shocking sight. So much greed. So much stealing. And all the brainchild of one lampless Genie.

'Come in, you two Mummies, your time is up,' Ali Pali announced through the megaphone, adding, 'OK, you can go in now,' to a waiting Banshee with a small handcart. Not surprisingly he was feeling very pleased with himself. All his carefully laid plans were bearing fruit. Why, shortly he'd have enough for that nice little solid silver number he'd always had his eye on. The one with the twirly handle and that elegant spout. The one he'd always fancied. By the end of the night, he'd have enough to buy it outright. If his luck held.

'What's goin' on 'ere then? What you doin' wiv the rubbish?' enquired a passing Zombie from another wood, squinting curiously into the tent. (Zombies are almost as dense as Goblins.)

'I'm cleaning up,' explained Ali Pali, and laughed until he choked.

CHAPTER THIRTEEN
Treachery

Can you imagine this scene from the air? All the lights and noise and bustle? And can you imagine the effect such a spectacle might have on a posse of twelve well meaning AWOL Broomsticks who have come sick-visiting?

On the whole, the Brooms had had a smooth flight. A bit of minor turbulence here and there, and a small detour to buy a Get Well card and grapes, but otherwise uneventful. Until they got a bit closer to their destination, that is, and suddenly became aware of *a mysterious glow in the sky*! It appeared to be coming from Pongwiffy's rubbish dump up ahead. Instant panic.

Huh? Glow in the sky? Where? How? Why? What?

Understandably, the Broomsticks were feeling a bit jittery. Bear in mind that they are a law-abiding sort who don't even break the speed limit often, let alone go sneaking off on wild mercy errands without permission. The long, cold flight had done wonders to dampen their enthusiasm. They were already wishing they hadn't come. Already anxious to get back before someone spotted they were missing. Quite honestly, a mysterious glow was something they could have done without. However, having come this far, the Brooms felt duty bound to investigate. Slowly, hesitantly, keeping close together, they approached The Dump and peered down.

Nothing could have prepared them for the shock. They were instantly thrown into confusion. They came to a ragged halt, skittered about a bit, then bobbed unsteadily in mid-air, skulking behind the odd wispy bit of cloud and trying to blend in with the treetops. Eyes on stalks, they goggled disbelievingly at the scene below. A sudden puff of wind tugged one of Ali Pali's posters from a tree trunk and hurled it skywards. It got all tangled up with Stumpy's bristles. Stumpy didn't need to read it in order to twig what was going on.

The Dump had been invaded!

The ultimate crime.

Oooer.

Yes indeed, Pongwiffy's pride and joy was crawling with unsavoury riff-raff who actually appeared to be helping themselves! Oh, the bold blatancy of it! Lights, music, theft on a grand scale! Oh, the deceit of it! The sheer cheek of it! Whatever would Pongwiffy say?

The Brooms were terribly shocked. Not one of them had a clue what to do. Uncertainly they milled about, agitatedly scanning the ground below for any sign of Woody. It was hopeless. The garden shed appeared to have been taken over by a fortune-telling Gnome and Woody was nowhere to be seen. Their poor, suffering friend had most probably been carted off by some crazed rubbish-happy lout as part of his/her/its haul. Grapes and Get Well cards suddenly seemed inappropriate.

Far below, one of the Hell's Gnomes glanced up. Suddenly, hanging about seemed inappropriate as well.

'FLY FOR IT!'

As one, the Brooms turned, pointed towards Crag Hill and took off at a hundred miles per hour, screaming their bristles off. And that's why Pongwiffy, Hugo and Woody, flying along at a sedate five miles per hour, suddenly heard a faint whistling sound. Then, to their great dismay, they were faced with the unsettling sight of twelve stampeding Broomsticks heading straight towards them at incredible speed with no obvious intention of stopping.

'It's the Brooms! They've escaped from the Goblins! They're bolting! Emergency dive!' shrieked Pongwiffy, clutching on to her hat. And Woody did. Only just in time.

Whooooooooosh!

With a blast of wind, the Broomsticks passed overhead, missing them by a whisker.

'Phew! Vell done, Broom. Zat vas a near vun!' remarked Hugo as the three of them clung precariously to the sharp top of a pine tree.

Woody said nothing. It was still recovering from

the shock. After all it had been through, being forced so rudely out of the sky by its own mates was the very last straw.

For once, Pongwiffy had nothing to say either. Mainly because she had a small branch in her mouth, but also because she was so very depressed. Everything seemed to be going wrong. Oh, why oh why did all this have to happen when she should be putting her mind to fund-raising for the Hallowe'en party? It just wasn't fair.

'Come on, Mistress, cheer up,' coaxed Hugo. 'Look on ze bright side. Ve find ze Brooms, ya? So! Ze main problem is solved. And ve still in vun piece. And I 'ave plan.'

'You do?' said Pongwiffy, perking up. 'What is it?'

'Ve go 'ome,' said Hugo. 'Ve climb down zis tree, valk to ze 'ovel and ave a nice cuppa bogwater. Ve cannot be far from 'ome. I pretty sure it over zere, look. Near zat glow in sky.'

He waved his paw in a vague southerly direction. Both Pongwiffy and Woody brightened up.

'Agreed,' said Pongwiffy. 'Tonight's been one long disaster from beginning to end. A nice hot cuppa will do us all the world of good. You go down first, Hugo. Then if I fall, at least one of my feet will have something soft to land on.'

'OK. I go now – but vait! Vat zat?'

'What's what? By the way, I've been thinking. *What glow in the sky?*'

'Sssssh!' hissed Hugo. 'Look!'

Silently, he pointed below. Pongwiffy looked down – and nearly fell off her branch in shock. Passing below the very tree in which they perched, shuffled two Mummies. Moonlight glinted off their bandages. Everyone knew them, because they were the only Mummies for a thousand miles. As thieves, they were at a very distinct disadvantage.

'Ees Xotindis and Xstufitu,' breathed Hugo. 'And, Mistress, look! Look vat zey carry!'

Between them, Xotindis and Xstufitu carried a sofa. But not just any sofa. Oh no. This sofa, until very recently, had enjoyed pride of place in Pongwiffy's own living room! It was the nastiest sofa that anyone could ever dream up in their wildest nightmares. It was exceptionally awful when new, but you should have seen it after Pongwiffy had had it for a few years. It was stained with sloppings and crisp with crumbs. Three springs burst out of the seat. It was old and disgusting, and

Pongwiffy loved it.

'AHHHHHHHHHHHHHH! MY SOFA! MINE! STOP, THIEF!'

Flustered night birds rose flapping from the trees as the outraged squawk echoed through the Wood. The Mummies instantly recognised who it was, and broke into a panicky run. They did quite well. It's no easy thing to run through a wood with a stolen sofa if you're swathed in bandages and completely blind. They managed at least three steps before Xotindis (the one at the back) caught his toe in a root. Both fell down with a crash and began to unravel.

'Are you all right, Otto?' asked Xstufitu in a muffled voice.

'Not sure yet. What about you, Stufi?' came the reply.

'I think I'm OK. Come on, let's crawl for it!'

'Not so fast, you!'

Pongwiffy placed her foot firmly on the end of Xstufitu's bandage. 'Don't move, or you're unwound!'

'It's a fair cop,' said Xstufitu, sitting up and rubbing his elbow. 'Get your foot off my bandage, Pongwiffy. It isn't funny to mess with a Mummy's bandages.'

'It's not a fair cop, Stufi,' objected Xotindis. 'We paid good money to get this sofa. It's ours now, Pongwiffy.'

'Do you hear that?' remarked Pongwiffy to Hugo and Woody. 'Can you believe a walking strip of old rag could tell such shocking lies?'

'Watch it,' snapped Xotindis. 'We were Pharaohs once, you know. You should mind how you address royalty, Pongwiffy.'

'I don't know about addressing royalty,' said Pongwiffy grimly, 'but I know how to *undress* royalty. I'm going to sit on MY sofa and listen while you two talk. You've got two minutes to tell me exactly what's been going on behind my back. Otherwise, consider yourself unravelled.'

Xotindis and Xstufitu looked at each other, and shrugged.

'Weellll,' began Xotindis slowly. 'There's this Genie . . .'

CHAPTER FOURTEEN
The Reunion

'Talk about a mess,' said Stinkwart, shaking his head. 'One of our worst flops, that.'

'I fink I've lost my hat,' said Lardo. He had been vainly searching his head for the last five minutes, and was pretty sure that the hat wasn't there. But the rest of the Goblins weren't especially interested.

They were huddled in the bushes bordering the empty Broom park, eating humbugs and arguing about what had gone wrong. The quarrel had started immediately after the botched raid, and was still continuing.

'I still say it wuz all Plugugly's fault,' said Slop-bucket meanly, for the hundredth time.

''Ear! 'Ear!' agreed Stinkwart, Hog, Eyesore and Sproggit, also for the hundredth time.

'The fing is, wuz I wearin' it when I come out tonight?' pondered Lardo.

'Plugugly's a failure,' observed Eyesore. 'You're a failure, Plugugly.'

'I said I wuz sorry,' mumbled Plugugly sulkily. He was slumped dejectedly under a blackberry bush, gnawing at his thumbnail in a crestfallen manner. 'It were the stress.'

'We shoulda chopped it up,' insisted young Sproggit. 'Chopped it up, like I said in the first place. Shouldn't we, Lardo?'

But Lardo was still concerned about his hat. He had a horrible feeling it had fallen off in the Broom park and was even now lying there in the moonlight for anyone to see. (It was. One of the essential parts of any failed undercover Goblin mission is the leaving of at least one whacking great clue.)

'I'm fed up wiv sittin' 'ere,' said Slopbucket suddenly. 'I'm cold. I wanna go 'ome.'

'I'm cold too. No hat, see,' remarked Lardo,

pointing to his lumpy bare head. Everyone ignored him. So Lardo snatched Sproggit's hat and put it on his own head. Sproggit, of course, objected, and a brief fight followed. Everyone joined in out of habit, but nobody's heart was really in it.

Hog broke up the fight by passing round the humbugs, and for a short time the Goblins sat in silence, blowing hot, humbuggy breath on their cold fingers and trying not to think about the long walk home.

That was when Macabre (following a hunch) arrived at the Broom park for the first time. She was so shocked to find it deserted that she didn't notice the Goblins in the bushes. She did notice Lardo's hat, though. She swooped down on it with a cry of triumph and bore it away at full gallop.

'What were that?' asked Hog. 'Sounded like gallopin' hooves.'

'Probably a squirrel,' said Eyesore knowledgeably. ''Ave a look, Sproggit.'

Sproggit crawled off into the bushes. He lost his way and was gone quite a long time. When he finally crawled back, the rest of the Goblins had dozed off. Sproggit shrugged, then joined them.

When Macabre returned to the Broom park to

303

hunt for clues more thoroughly, she wondered how she had missed them the first time. There they were, right next to the scene of the crime, all snoring like mad and reeking of peppermint. Scattered all around them was the evidence of a full-scale Broomnapping attempt. Of the Brooms there was still no sign.

Macabre hugged herself with excitement. She dismounted from Rory and tiptoed over to the sleeping Goblins. Then:

'Wakey wakey!' screeched Macabre, and treated them to a deafening blast on her bagpipes. At the same time Rory let fire with a malicious moo. The Goblins stirred, sat up and blearily knuckled their eyes.

'Stand and deliver! Surrender! Hands oop!' Macabre had a bossy sort of nature, and loved arresting people. In fact, she always carried a pair of handcuffs in her sporran, in case she ever got the chance to use them. Delightedly, she clapped them on Plugugly, then tied up the rest of the Goblins with rope whilst they were still half asleep. She then frogmarched them away from the Broom park, down the hill and into the enemy camp.

'Now, look what Ah got! Goblins!' bellowed Macabre importantly. 'Caught napping at the scene o' the crime, they were. Skulking in yon bushes. Aye. Broomnappers. Every last one.'

Seven sleepy, surly Goblins were rudely thrust forward. The assembled Witches gave them the usual charming Witch welcome: they pulled rude faces, jeered, and pelted the captives with bread rolls. Ratsnappy stuck her foot out to trip up Lardo and Bendyshanks poked Eyesore in the leg with a stick. Sludgegooey dabbled her fingers in her mug of tepid bogwater and flicked some in Plugugly's eye. Sproggit got jostled. Stinkwart got hit in the ear with a piece of ham. The Witches were having a wonderful time. What a night it had been. First, the business of Pongwiffy's Broom. That was closely followed by the excitement of the Broomnapping. Then there was the discovery that their Magic wasn't working properly and the State Of Emergency and everything. Now, just when things were beginning to get dull, hey presto! The Broomnappers themselves turn up! The sandwiches were getting low, but the Witches' spirits were running high.

'Boo!'

'Go home, Plugugly!'

'Stand up straight, Slopbucket, you'll trip over your knuckles!'

'What you lot done with our Brooms then, maggot face?'

'Let me through! Let me at 'em! I'm Grandwitch, I get to ask the questions!' shouted Sourmuddle, pushing her way through the crowd to where the Goblins stood in a truculent huddle. Macabre stood to attention and saluted proudly as the boss hobbled up.

'Well done, Macabre. Glad to see somebody's got their wits about them. Right, you Goblins. What have you got to say for yourselves? Caught red-handed, eh?'

'We din do nuffin',' chanted the Goblins automatically.

'Don't be ridiculous. Of course you did.'

'Indubitably!' agreed Greymatter. 'Place them in detention! Incarcerate them!'

'Make 'em walk the plank!' (Dead Eye Dudley, former pirate cat.)

'Guilty! Guilty!' (Everybody else.)

'We din do nuffin'!' chorused the Goblins again. It was what they always said when they were caught red-handed. It was a response guaranteed to irritate, particularly when they kept saying it. A lot of hissing and growling and gnashing of teeth and so on came from the crowd. Barry the Vulture flapped up to a tree, hunched his shoulders and adopted what he liked to think of as his Threatening Pose. Snoop the Demon tested his pitchfork for sharpness. Gaga's bats jostled and squeaked angrily. There was the ominous sound of claw sharpening.

The Goblins flinched and cowered. It looked as if things were going to get nasty.

'Oh, come now,' snapped Sourmuddle, enjoying herself. 'Of course you've got our Brooms. You've hidden them somewhere. You're at our mercy. You might as well tell us where they are. Come along, come along.'

'We ain't got yer stoopid Brooms,' muttered Sproggit. 'If you must know, they flewed off on their own. We din do nuffin'.'

'Oooh, what a fibber!'

'Just flew off, did he say? Our Brooms? A likely story!'

'Turn 'im into a frog, Sourmuddle. Make an example of 'im!'

Sproggit shrugged and tried to pretend he didn't care. Actually he didn't much. Frog spells always wore off in time. Sooner or later he'd end up a Goblin again. What were a few days of forced swimming and mayflies for breakfast in the great scheme of things? But it didn't come to that anyway, because:

'Hold it, girls! Do you see what I see?' said Bendyshanks suddenly, through a mouthful of sandwich. And she pointed upwards. Everyone – Witches, Familiars and Goblins – turned their attention to the sky. All mouths dropped open.

The sky was full of Brooms! They whizzed about overhead, obviously preparing for touchdown.

'They're back!' went up the surprised cry. 'Our Brooms are back!'

'That's funny,' said Sourmuddle. 'I wonder where they've been? Looks like you Goblins didn't have 'em after all. You arrested 'em for nothing, Macabre. What a pity, eh?'

Macabre was lying full length on the ground, pummelling it with her fists, and didn't reply.

'Told you,' chorused the Goblins. 'We din do nuffin'. Told you.' And Plugugly added, 'Dey flewed away, like Sproggit said. So yah boo sucks to you, Macabre.'

Just then, Sharkadder came hurrying up. After spending virtually the whole of this book on bad terms with Pongwiffy, she was finally beginning to come round. It was the look on Pongwiffy's face when she flew off all on her own. All hurt and forlorn. Sharkadder had almost called her back and said she'd go with her, but she'd had an egg roll in her mouth at the time and couldn't. Now she felt bad. Pongwiffy was awful, but best friends were best friends.

'Where's Pong?' asked Sharkadder, scanning the sky. 'Why isn't she with them?'

'Who knows?' said Sourmuddle, unconcerned. 'Who cares? I tell you what, there's something funny about those Brooms.'

She was right. Just at that moment, the Brooms touched down. It wasn't a neat, orderly touchdown. As touchdowns go, it was a mess. There was a hasty, hysterical quality about it. There was a lot of flurried skidding and bumping and misjudgement. And you only had to look at the Brooms' stricken expressions to know that they were upset about something. They jiggled up and down and pointed urgently to the sky.

'Oh dear,' groaned Sourmuddle. 'Not again. It's like a horrible recurring nightmare. They're trying to warn us about something. I don't suppose anyone . . . ?'

No. No one was prepared to speak Wood.

'Not even for the sake of National Security?' coaxed Sourmuddle.

Not even for that. As one, the Witches folded their arms, tapped their feet and suddenly became fascinated by their own dirty fingernails.

Meanwhile, the Brooms ran around in small circles, wringing their hands helplessly and getting in a terrible tizzy.

'Well, someone's got to find out what they're on about, and it won't be me,' insisted Sourmuddle. 'Because I'm boss. Come along. A volunteer to speak Wood. I'm not sitting through charades again.'

'I'll do it,' said Sharkadder, suddenly stepping forward. 'I'll do it for the sake of Pongwiffy, because despite everything, she's my best friend.'

Dead Eye Dudley spat disgustedly.

'Well, I'm sorry, Duddles, but she is,' insisted Sharkadder. 'And I'm sure you wouldn't *really* want anything awful to happen to Hugo.'

'Yes I would,' said Dudley.

'We've all forgotten something,' remarked Greymatter. 'Our Magic's still not working. I don't suppose you can even remember the spell,

Sharkadder. Can anyone remember that language spell? The one with the side effects? I'm sure I can't.'

Greymatter was right. No one could. Mind you, no one tried very hard.

'Me neither,' said Sharkadder, trying not to sound too relieved. 'That's that, then.'

'No more charades!' repeated Sourmuddle firmly. 'Too boring. Takes too long. Look, I've had enough excitement for one night. Personally, I'm for cancelling the State of Emergency and going home. Whatever the important message is, it can probably wait until tomorrow . . .'

'Wait! Look what I've found! This explains everything!'

Sludgegooey was urgently waving the poster which she had just discovered entangled in Stumpy's bristles. Very sensibly, Stumpy had hung on to it. In fact, Stumpy had been trying to draw her attention to it for some time, but Sludgegooey was a bit slow on the uptake.

'Listen!' said Sludgegooey. And read it out.

There was an instant's shocked silence, then a howl of rage went up! The Brooms, limp with relief, sagged against trees and fanned themselves. It took a while for the Goblins' slow brains to grasp the significance of the words on the poster – but when they did, they started kicking themselves for missing the sale of the century. Just think. All that effort wasted on a failed Broomnapping when they could have strolled along to The Dump and helped themselves to as much rubbish as they could carry for a fiver.

'So that's it!' said Sourmuddle. 'Genie Enterprises, eh? I should have guessed. Only a Genie would have the cheek. In the words of my old mother, never trust a flashy dresser, especially if he lives in a lamp. Mind you, I'm surprised a Genie would have the skill to dismantle that Wall of Pongwiffy's. I've never put much store by that gaudy oriental Magic myself. Oh well. You live and learn.'

At long last, all was clear. Except that nobody was very sure how the Goblins fitted in. Or why the Brooms had gone off all by themselves. Or where Pongwiffy was. Or who was the mastermind behind Genie Enterprises, and how was he able to work such an elaborate fiddle unless he'd had inside help? Come to think of it, all wasn't clear by a long way.

'Well, one thing's certain,' continued Sourmuddle. 'This here Genie Enterprises isn't getting away with it. We'll go and sort him out. RIGHT NOW.'

'Whoopee!' bellowed Macabre, brightening up. Eagerly, she began stuffing stale bread rolls into her sporran for ammunition.

'Witches, to your Broomsticks!' ordered Sourmuddle. 'Last one on's a goody-goody!'

The Witches didn't need telling twice (except for Bonidle, who had to be told several times). They vaulted on to their Broomsticks. There was a drone of bagpipes, discordant wails on violins, and the sound of knuckles cracking. Then, with a good selection of wild cackling cries, they rose into the sky.

'Tally-ho!' shrieked Sourmuddle as her Broomstick plunged and reared, as over-excited as a highly strung racehorse. 'Follow me, girls! To The Dump!'

'To The Dump, to The Dump, to The Dump, Dump, Dump!' sang everybody, and seconds later, they were gone. Plugugly, Stinkwart, Hog, Slopbucket, Lardo, Eyesore and Sproggit were left behind, still tied up but not so tight that they couldn't shuffle over and eat the remains of the sandwiches.

CHAPTER FIFTEEN
The Battle For The Dump

The Battle For The Dump has, of course, passed into Witch folklore. That's because the Witches won. (Battles which the Witches lose tend not to pass into folklore. They pass into oblivion.) The Battle For The Dump, being a victory, got talked about and mulled over and relived for months afterwards. Tactics were discussed. Personal acts of heroism and bravery were trotted out again and again by Witches, Familiars and Brooms alike. Everyone claimed a stunning – no, let's be honest, *unbelievable* – personal success rate. To hear every-

314

one talk, you'd have thought that she, he or it had won the entire battle alone and unaided.

The Battle For The Dump began as Ali Pali was stuffing yet more bundles of five-pound notes into his carpet bag. He was on his second cash register, having worn out the first. What a night it had been! His bag was bursting at the seams. Most of the choice pieces of rubbish had been snapped up long ago – yet still the punters came. Just as Ali Pali would think the crowds were thinning a little, and wonder whether he ought to think of packing up and clearing out, more eager junk hunters would arrive waving fistfuls of fivers, desperate to wade in.

A whole crowd of Vampires (bonfire fangatics all) were bussed in. So rife was the spirit of competition, some of the keener types went home to get another fiver and *had more than the one go*! The tea hut was doing a roaring trade, and the badge seller had run out. A steady stream of rubbish poured out of The Dump, which by now was beginning to look sadly depleted.

'Rubbish Fever,' thought Ali Pali with a superior little chuckle. 'That's what they've got. Junk on the brain. Bonfire crazy, the poor saps.'

(Genies don't go in for Hallowe'en. They feel

315

they're much too sophisticated to jump around bonfires on chilly hills. If they celebrate it at all, it's likely to be lying on some silken couch eating grapes, or an intimate little supper party in some friend's lamp.)

Ali Pali certainly had cause for celebration. Everything had gone so smoothly. Dismantling the Wall of Smell had been simple, because Pongwiffy had given him the recipe (and once you have the recipe, you can easily work out the antidote). Jamming the Witches' magic signals just in case they tried to 'ring home', as it were, had been a masterstroke. The information had come straight out of Pongwiffy's own secret Magical code books. And as for the transformation of The Dump – well, it was beyond question the best thing he had ever done.

'Rich!' crowed Ali to himself. 'Rich beyond my wildest dreams! I think I'll skip the lamp and go straight for the palace!'

His smug little chuckle turned into a great, triumphant cackle. No more of that Your Wish Is My Command stuff. He could retire. Why, if he wanted, he could afford his *own* Genie! Then, as is often the way, something happened to spoil it all.

'Excuse me, Mr Pali,' said a voice. It was the Thing in the Moonmad T-shirt. 'I think you got company,' it said. And pointed up. Ali Pali looked and gave a little whistle. The night sky was suddenly full of screaming Witches. Even as he looked, they banked steeply, grouped into battle formation and prepared to attack.

'Oh-oh. Closing time, I think,' said Ali Pali, snapping his fingers at his carpet bag, which immediately yawned open. Quickly and efficiently, he began to pack.

As he did so, the screaming Witches swooped down upon The Dump like angry hornets, buzzing the unsuspecting punters and making them scatter in all directions. Some dropped to the ground and hid their heads. Others took to their heels and ran into the trees for cover, getting away with whatever they could. A few put up a token resistance, but the Witches had the advantage of surprise, so there wasn't much point. By far the most sensible course was to drop the loot and scarper. Fast.

Quite a few made it to safety. The Hell's Gnomes had their bikes, and made a clean getaway. So did the Trolls, the Yetis, the fortune-telling Gnome and the Thing with the Moonmad T-shirt. The Skeletons regretfully abandoned the last of Pongwiffy's chair legs, piled into their hearse, and drove off with an impressive screaming of brakes.

Others weren't so lucky. The Ghouls were terribly slow movers. Every time they struggled to their knees they'd get buzzed again, and would slowly topple head first into The Dump to yet another mouthful of something awful. And they weren't the only unlucky ones. When it came to ham roll throwing, Macabre was mustard. Many a Dump raider staggered home with hot ears and black eyes that night. Others got pinched, scratched or had their hair pulled. One of the Werewolves got flapped at most unpleasantly by a bunch of Bats. The greediest Troll received a nasty peck from Barry. A Banshee got clonked by a Broomstick and needed a plaster.

Safe in his stripy tent, Ali Pali scooped up the last of the loot. His plan was to vanish instantly and as discreetly as possible (no green smoke and no bang). He would make for some quiet, oriental haven and go underground for a bit, until the heat died down. Then, as soon as everyone had forgotten or ceased to care, he and his carpet bag would emerge, head for the nearest estate agent and spend, spend, spend!

That was the plan, anyway. And it might have worked too, if only he had been just that little bit quicker. He had just snapped the bulging carpet bag shut, and was looking round the tent to make sure he hadn't forgotten anything, when he heard a noise behind him. He whirled round and came face to face with . . .

Pongwiffy! Behind her, twiggy arms folded menacingly, stood her Broom, and on her shoulder perched the most ferocious-looking Hamster Ali had ever seen in his life.

Ali Pali noticed several things. He noticed that Pongwiffy was holding an extremely perky-looking Wand. In her other hand she held a small, green, ominous bottle. He also noticed uncomfortably that she was smiling.

'Hello, Ali,' purred Pongwiffy. 'Going somewhere?'

Much, much later, after all the fun was over and everyone had gone home, a Gaggle of Goblins trailed through Witchway Wood. They were pushing a squeaking cart full of ropes, pitchforks, nets, and so on. They looked just about all in. It had taken them ages to bite through Macabre's knots and free themselves. Then they'd had to drag themselves back to the Broom park to pick up all their equipment. Then they'd set off on the long walk home.

What a scene of carnage greeted them as they squeaked along under the trees. Wonderingly, they stared around. At the crashed wardrobe. At the abandoned mangle. At the dropped newspapers. At that thoroughly awful sofa. Everywhere there were pieces of garbage and scattered bread rolls. All pointing to a hasty flight.

'Must 'ave bin some punch-up,' said Slopbucket, awed.

'Yer,' agreed Sproggit, rubbing his eyes blearily. 'An' we missed it.'

'I wonder who won?' yawned Lardo.

'The Witches, of course,' said Hog. 'They always do. I wonder why that is?'

'Well, one fing's fer sure,' said Eyesore with a sneer. 'They won't be the only ones wiv a good bonfire this year. Looks like the uvvers got away wiv a pile o' stuff. Yerp, there'll be some good blazes this Hallowe'en.'

''Cept fer ours, o' course,' put in Stinkwart. 'It's

all your fault, Plugugly.'

But something was the matter with Plugugly. His eyes were rolling wildly and his face had gone very red. Funny, strangled noises were coming from his mouth. Finally, he spoke.

'I fink – wait, it's comin' – lads, I fink I got anudder idear!'

There was alarmed consternation from the other Goblins. Cries of 'Oh no, anyfing but that!'

'No, reelly, wait a tick, I 'ave, I reelly 'ave. An' it's simple. Listen, we got de cart, right? An' dere's no one about. An' dere's all dis rubbish lying around, right? Now den. *What's ter stop us pickin' it up an' takin' it 'ome?*'

He was right. There was nothing to stop them. It was a brilliant plan, and exactly what they did. They also collected up the bread rolls. So fans of the Goblins will be delighted to know that at least something turned out right for them that night.

CHAPTER SIXTEEN
Friends Again

One week later. The sun rose early on the morning of Hallowe'en – but not as early as Witch Sharkadder. When day dawned crisp and clear, she had already been hard at work for a good hour. She was seated before her mirror in a pink dressing gown, Getting Ready. Her head bristled with hedgehog hair rollers, and she was waiting for her mud pack to dry. Now and then, she took careful, dainty sips from a bowl of mouseli. The party was that very night, and she did like to take her time on these special occasions. Only nineteen hours to go, when all was said and done.

She was enjoying herself tremendously, because she had a whole new range of sinister little pots to play with. Pongwiffy had bought them for her, like the good friend she was. (What Sharkadder didn't know was that Pongwiffy had paid for them with her Magic Coin, the one which always ends up back in her own purse. In fact, there was going to be quite a bit of trouble about the new range of make-up – but that's another story.)

Sharkadder was determined to do a particularly magnificent job. It was essential that she should get the make-up just right for the Fancy Dress parade. In her dual role as judge and participant, she owed it to the rest of them to show how it should be done.

Getting the new make-up and being reinstated as judge had all been part of making friends with Pongwiffy again. They have been best friends now for a record time. Seven days. Ever since The Night Of The Battle, as it came to be called. (Although Sharkadder thought of it more as The Night Of Our Last Row. And the Coal Shovel and Rake referred to it as The Night We Got Slung Out Of Our Own Shed. And Woody thought of it as The Night Of My Great Shame. And Plugugly thought of it as

De Night I 'Ad All Dem Idears. And Bendyshanks' snake, Slithering Steve, thought of it as The Night I Learned To Do A Reef Knot. It just depended on your point of view, really.)

Anyway. If the truth be known, Sharkadder felt rather badly about that night. Yes, Pongwiffy had behaved stupidly, but that was nothing new. She, Sharkadder, hadn't really helped matters. She had been generally unforgiving and not at all helpful to a friend in need. Poor old Pong. Everything had gone wrong for her. All right, so it all worked out in the end, and they had come out of the whole thing with oodles of money, but it had been a terrible price to pay. Pongwiffy's view from her hovel window had changed. The Dump, once a vision of mouldering loveliness, was a shadow of its former self. Pongwiffy was deeply attached to her rubbish, and it would take her a long time to get over such a great loss. Luckily, arrangements for the party had taken her mind off things.

'Dear old Pong,' thought Sharkadder, coming over all sentimental. She looked fondly over at the magnificent costume, hired at considerable expense, now hanging in splendour from a hook. Sharkadder hadn't hesitated in choosing what she was going as.

She was going as the Wicked Queen in Snow White. It was a lifetime's ambition. She couldn't wait to put it all on, especially the dress. As she thought of wearing That Dress, she almost allowed an excited grin to crack her face – but that would never do. The mud pack didn't really allow for smiling. Time for the nails now. They had to be filed to points and painted blood red. As soon as they were dry, oh goody goody, she could put the dress on! She picked up the file, and carefully, oh so carefully, began to rub. Then:

'Yoo-hoo! Sharky! It's me, Pongwiffy. Can I come in?'

Sharkadder leapt a mile in the air and two tragic things happened. Her mud pack cracked and she broke a nail.

'Morning,' said Pongwiffy, bustling in, making for the kettle. 'I can't stay, I'm far too busy. I just popped by to wish my very best friend a Happy Hallowe'en. I meant to buy you a present, but you know how it is. Oooh! Mouseli. My favourite cereal.'

Sharkadder got herself under control with difficulty. She bit her lip and reached for the glue, reminding herself of the seven-day

325

friendship record.

'All right, Pong, you've said hello,' she said. 'Now go. I don't want you hanging round here all morning. Not when I'm Getting Ready.'

'I'm ready already,' said Pongwiffy, who looked exactly the same as usual. 'I'm absolutely ready. I'm the Witch from Hansel and Gretel. The one with the house of sweets.'

'But you look exactly the same as always,' said Sharkadder.

'No I don't,' said Pongwiffy. 'If you look carefully, you'll notice several boiled sweets stuck around the hem of my skirt. There were more, but I keep eating them.'

Sharkadder shrugged. It didn't really matter what anyone else wore, as long as she was the Wicked Queen. In That Dress. 'How's your Broom?' she asked, just to be polite.

'Much better, thanks. I left it outside with yours. With strict instructions not to go flying off on its own again.'

(Indeed, Woody was slowly recovering with the aid of its fellow Brooms, who had formed a support group. The general feeling seemed to be that, whilst it didn't exactly deserve an award for distinguished service, it didn't need its nose rubbed in it either. Woody fans will be pleased to know that within a couple of days it stopped jumping at every noise, and within a week it had forgotten the entire incident. So had the rest of them. Brooms have long, thin brains that don't leave much room for memory.)

'And how are the party arrangements going?' asked Sharkadder as she attempted to fix her ruined nail.

'Oh, fine, fine. Everything's under control. We start off with the Fancy Dress parade on the dot of midnight. I've booked the Witchway Rhythm Boys and they'll play marching music while we all walk round in our costumes. Pierre de Gingerbeard's doing the cake. He's expensive, but money's no object this year.'

'Good old Pierre,' nodded Sharkadder. 'He's my cousin, you know.'

'I know. You've told me a million times. Oh, and I've hired the Yetis to run the barbecue. Macabre's in charge of the games. Ratsnappy's bringing the funny hats. Gaga's crackers, as usual. I've got Scrofula putting the chocolate spiders into the party bags. The entertainment's all organised. Agglebag and Bagaggle will do a violin recital, I'm afraid, and Macabre's insisting on playing her bagpipes, but Sludgegooey's promised to try to hide them. I've cut Greymatter's poetry reading down to thirty seconds. I've booked a conjuror and a tap-dancing Dwarf and a singing Leprechaun. Oh, and some Gnome who tells fortunes. It's going to be the best party in Witch History.'

'Sounds lovely,' said Sharkadder. 'I can't wait.'

'The only thing that won't be up to scratch is the bonfire,' said Pongwiffy with a sigh. 'To be frank, I'm ashamed of it. But we all know who to thank for *that*, don't we?'

'We certainly do,' agreed Sharkadder. 'I was going to ask you about him. What did you do with him? In the end?'

'What do you think? I bottled him,' said Pongwiffy grimly. 'He works for me now.'

'Oh, what a good idea,' said Sharkadder, clapping her hands. 'Are you finding him useful?'

'Yes and no,' said Pongwiffy. And from a pocket in her cardigan, she produced the small, ominous green bottle with an ill-fitting cork stuffed in the top to keep it stoppered. You didn't have to be a Genie to know it would be cramped in there and probably very stuffy. Pongwiffy tossed it casually on to the table.

'Go on, spit in it if you like. I do, often. He's not in right now. I've sent him off to Crag Hill to do the party decorations. That'll teach him to interfere with Walls Of Smell that I build. Hugo's gone to keep an eye on him.'

'Why?' asked Sharkadder. 'You think he'll try to escape?'

'Oh no. It's just to make sure he gets the decorations right. He's good at transformations, I'll grant you that, but everything he does always has that *tinselly* sort of look. I keep telling him. Gloomier, I say. Easy on the fairy lights. Forget the incense. This is a Witch party, and we Witches don't go in for all those cheap special effects.'

'How does he like the accommodation?' asked Sharkadder with a sneer. 'Not up to his usual standards, I suppose?'

'He does nothing but moan. I'm freeing him after the party. It's all very well having a slave to do all the work, but every time he appears he's got a list of complaints as long as your arm. He's threatening me with the Genies' Union now. He reckons I'm only entitled to three wishes by law, then I have to

release him.'

They both sighed and shook their heads.

'What a cheek,' they tutted in chorus.

'What's even worse,' confided Pongwiffy, lowering her voice, 'what's even *more* worrying, he says he'll spread it around that I – you know – told him about our secret code numbers and gave him the recipe for the Wall Of Smell.'

'Well, of course, he's right,' Sharkadder was quick to point out. 'It was all your own fault, Pong.'

'I know, I know,' said Pongwiffy uncomfortably. 'I thought we weren't going to talk about that. You promised you wouldn't tell.'

'Of course I won't,' said Sharkadder stoutly. 'I'm your best friend, remember?'

'Still,' said Pongwiffy, brightening up, 'things could have been worse. At least I caught him before he made off with the money. And you and I are friends again. And the Broom's better. And none of us had to speak Wood. And tonight we're going to have the best Hallowe'en party in the history of the universe!'

'And I'm going to be the Wicked Queen,' added Sharkadder.

'So you are, so you are. And with that costume

and your looks, I'm sure you'll have no hesitation in awarding yourself first prize in the Fancy Dress.'

'Oh, I will,' agreed Sharkadder confidently. 'Thanks, Pong.'

'You're welcome,' said Pongwiffy. 'Er – any chance of breakfast?'

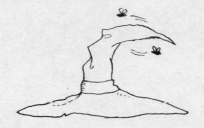

Post Script

For those of you who like to know these things, here are a few details.

The Witches' Party
Highly successful. Unanimously voted Best Hallowe'en Party Yet. Here are the results of the *Fancy Dress parade*:

1st Prize:
The Wicked Queen from Snow White and her Faithful Cat (Sharkadder and Dudley)

2nd Prize:
Little Bo Peep (Sourmuddle. Snoop declined to be a sheep)

3rd Prize:
Joan of Arc and her Trusty Steed (Macabre and Rory)

Runners-up:
Tweedledee and Tweedledum (Ag and Bag)

Highly Commended:
Gaga, for her highly individual interpretation of a storm in a teacup.

No mention at all of:
Happy the Dwarf (Ratsnappy)
The Good Witch Glinda (Sludgegooey)
The Witches on the Blasted Heath (Greymatter, Bendyshanks and Scrofula)
Sleeping Beauty and Friend (Bonidle and the Sloth)
The Sweet House Witch (Pongwiffy)

Judges:
Sharkadder, Ali Pali (who was uncorked for the

evening) and one of the Witchway Rhythm Boys (a small Dragon named Arthur).

Sharkadder, Sourmuddle, Macabre, Agglebag and Bagaggle and Gaga thought the results exceptionally fair. Everyone else disagreed. So, as well as all the other lovely things that were laid on, Pongwiffy's famed Hallowe'en Party included an enjoyable little punch-up towards the end. Everyone agreed that the bonfire wasn't quite up to scratch this year, though.

Other Snippets of Information:

The Goblins had their best ever Hallowe'en. Not only was their bonfire huge, they had all those bread rolls. Plus, the Witches sent over a crate of past-the-sell-by-date blackcurrant brew as a gesture of ill will. To the Goblins, who live mostly on salt-flavoured water and boiled nettles, it tasted lovely.

Ali Pali took advantage of the fight that broke out after the Fancy Dress parade, and got away. The last time he was heard of, he was flogging second-hand flying carpets to Zombies, so the likelihood is that by now he is a very rich Genie indeed with a lamp in town and another one in the country.

Pongwiffy and Sharkadder broke friends again during the party. All over something Hugo said to Dudley. But that hardly comes as news, does it?

Greymatter's Poem (All thirty seconds)

What an entertaining, scintillating,
awe-inspiring party!
What a merry Celebration, what a spree!
What a cause for jubilation
Right across our great Witch nation!
What a nasty look Pongwiffy's giving me . . .

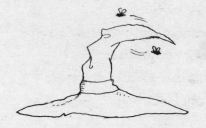

More Pongwiffy

coming soon!